MARK TWAIN'S

SHORT

STORIES

By: Mark Twain

This book has been published by:

Contact: sales@ezreads.net

URL: http://www.ezreads.net

Publishing Date: 2009

ISBN# 978-1-61534-093-4

Striving to be a leader in digital publishing. All of our books have been digitalized
and reformatted to be *EZ* to *Read* and available in Paperback, two types of
Hardcover and several eBook formats.

See our website for a wide range of subjects including most religions, philosophy,
historical, classical fiction, freemasonry, esoteric, and ancient texts.

CONTENTS

IN DEFENCE OF HARRIET SHELLEY

By: Mark Twain

In Defence of Harriet Shelley

CHAPTER I

I have committed sins, of course; but I have not committed enough of them to entitle me to the punishment of reduction to the bread and water of ordinary literature during six years when I might have been living on the fat diet spread for the righteous in Professor Dowden's Life of Shelley, if I had been justly dealt with.

During these six years I have been living a life of peaceful ignorance. I was not aware that Shelley's first wife was unfaithful to him, and that that was why he deserted her and wiped the stain from his sensitive honor by entering into soiled relations with Godwin's young daughter. This was all new to me when I heard it lately, and was told that the proofs of it were in this book, and that this book's verdict is accepted in the girls' colleges of America and its view taught in their literary classes.

In each of these six years multitudes of young people in our country have arrived at the Shelley-reading age. Are these six multitudes unacquainted with this life of Shelley? Perhaps they are; indeed, one may feel pretty sure that the great bulk of them are. To these, then, I address myself, in the hope that some account of this romantic historical fable and the fabulist's manner of constructing and adorning it may interest them.

First, as to its literary style. Our negroes in America have several ways of entertaining themselves which are not found among the whites anywhere. Among these inventions of theirs is one which is particularly popular with them. It is a competition in elegant deportment. They hire a hall and bank the spectators' seats in rising tiers along the two sides, leaving all the middle stretch of the floor free. A cake is provided as a prize for the winner in the competition, and a bench of experts in deportment is appointed to award it. Sometimes there are as many as fifty contestants, male and female, and five hundred spectators. One at a time the contestants enter, clothed regardless of expense in what each considers the perfection of style and taste, and walk down the vacant central space and back again with that multitude of critical eyes on them. All that the competitor knows of fine airs and graces he throws into his carriage, all that he knows of seductive expression he throws into his countenance. He may use all the helps he can devise: watch- chain to twirl with his fingers, cane to do graceful things with, snowy handkerchief to flourish and get artful effects out of, shiny new stovepipe hat to assist in his courtly bows; and the colored lady may have a fan to work up her effects with, and smile over and blush behind, and she may add other helps, according to her judgment. When the review by individual detail is over, a grand review of all the contestants in procession follows, with all the airs and graces and all the bowings and smirkings on exhibition at once, and this enables the bench of experts to make the necessary comparisons and arrive at a verdict. The successful competitor gets the prize which I have before mentioned, and an abundance of applause and envy along with it. The negroes have a name for this grave deportment-tournament; a name taken from the prize contended for. They call it a Cakewalk.

This Shelley biography is a literary cake-walk. The ordinary forms of speech are absent from it. All the pages, all the paragraphs, walk by sedately, elegantly, not to say mincingly, in their Sunday-best, shiny and sleek, perfumed, and with boutonnieres in their button-holes; it is rare to find even a chance sentence that has forgotten to dress. If the book wishes to tell us that Mary Godwin, child of sixteen, had known afflictions, the fact saunters forth in this nobby outfit: "Mary was herself not unlearned in the lore of pain"--meaning by that that she had not always traveled on asphalt; or, as some authorities would frame it, that she had "been there herself," a form which, while preferable to the book's form, is still not to be recommended. If the book wishes to tell us that Harriet Shelley hired a wet-nurse, that commonplace fact gets turned into a dancing-master, who does his professional bow before us in pumps and knee-breeches, with his fiddle under one arm and his crush-hat under the other, thus: "The beauty of Harriet's motherly relation to her babe was marred in Shelley's eyes by the introduction into his house of a hireling nurse to whom was delegated the mother's tenderest office."

This is perhaps the strangest book that has seen the light since Frankenstein. Indeed, it is a Frankenstein itself; a Frankenstein with the original infirmity supplemented by a new one; a Frankenstein with the reasoning faculty wanting. Yet it believes it can reason, and is always trying. It is not content to leave a mountain of fact standing in the clear sunshine, where the simplest reader can perceive its form, its details, and its relation to the rest of the landscape, but thinks it must help him examine it and understand it; so its drifting mind settles upon it with that intent, but always with one and the same result: there is a change of temperature and the mountain is hid in a fog. Every time it sets up a premise and starts to reason from it, there is a surprise in store for the reader. It is strangely nearsighted, cross-eyed, and purblind. Sometimes when a mastodon walks across the field of its vision it takes it for a rat; at other times it does not see it at all.

The materials of this biographical fable are facts, rumors, and poetry. They are connected together and harmonized by the help of suggestion, conjecture, innuendo, perversion, and semi-suppression.

The fable has a distinct object in view, but this object is not acknowledged in set words. Percy Bysshe Shelley has done something which in the case of other men is called a grave crime; it must be shown that in his case it is not that, because he does not think as other men do about these things.

Ought not that to be enough, if the fabulist is serious? Having proved that a crime is not a crime, was it worth while to go on and fasten the responsibility of a crime which was not a crime upon somebody else? What is the use of hunting down and holding to bitter account people who are responsible for other people's innocent acts?

Still, the fabulist thinks it a good idea to do that. In his view Shelley's first wife, Harriet, free of all offense as far as we have historical facts for guidance, must be held unforgivably responsible for her husband's innocent act in deserting her and taking up with another woman.

Any one will suspect that this task has its difficulties. Any one will divine that nice work is necessary here, cautious work, wily work, and that there is entertainment to be had in watching the magician do it. There is indeed entertainment in watching him. He arranges his facts, his rumors, and his poems on his table in full view of the house, and shows you that everything is there--no deception, everything fair and above board. And this is apparently true, yet there is a defect, for some of his best stock is hid in an appendix-basket behind the door, and you do not come upon it until the exhibition is over and the enchantment of your mind accomplished--as the magician thinks.

There is an insistent atmosphere of candor and fairness about this book which is engaging at first, then a little burdensome, then a trifle fatiguing, then progressively suspicious, annoying, irritating, and oppressive. It takes one some little time to find out that phrases which seem intended to guide the reader aright are there to mislead him; that phrases which seem intended to throw light are there to throw darkness; that phrases which seem intended to interpret a fact are there to misinterpret it; that phrases which seem intended to forestall prejudice are there to create it; that phrases which seem antidotes are poisons in disguise. The naked facts arrayed in the book establish Shelley's guilt in that one episode which disfigures his otherwise superlatively lofty and beautiful life; but the historian's careful and methodical misinterpretation of them transfers the responsibility to the wife's shoulders as he persuades himself. The few meagre facts of Harriet Shelley's life, as furnished by the book, acquit her of offense; but by calling in the forbidden helps of rumor, gossip, conjecture, insinuation, and innuendo he destroys her character and rehabilitates Shelley's--as he believes. And in truth his unheroic work has not been barren of the results he aimed at; as witness the assertion made to me that girls in the colleges of America are taught that Harriet Shelley put a stain upon her husband's honor, and that that was what stung him into repurifying himself by deserting her and his child and entering into scandalous relations with a school-girl acquaintance of his.

If that assertion is true, they probably use a reduction of this work in those colleges, maybe only a sketch outlined from it. Such a thing as that could be harmful and misleading. They ought to cast it out and put the whole book in its place. It would not deceive. It would not deceive the janitor.

All of this book is interesting on account of the sorcerer's methods and the attractiveness of some of his characters and the repulsiveness of the rest, but no part of it is so much so as are the chapters wherein he tries to think he thinks he sets forth the causes which led to Shelley's desertion of his wife in 1814.

Harriet Westbrook was a school-girl sixteen years old. Shelley was teeming with advanced thought. He believed that Christianity was a degrading and selfish superstition, and he had a deep and sincere desire to rescue one of his sisters from it. Harriet was impressed by his various philosophies and looked upon him as an intellectual wonder-- which indeed he was. He had an idea that she could give him valuable help in his scheme regarding his sister; therefore he asked her to correspond with him. She was quite willing. Shelley was not thinking of love, for he was just getting over a passion for his cousin, Harriet Grove, and just getting well steeped in one for Miss Hitchener, a school- teacher. What might happen to Harriet Westbrook before the letter- writing was ended did not enter his mind. Yet an older person could have made a good guess at it, for in person Shelley was as beautiful as an angel, he was frank, sweet, winning, unassuming, and so rich in unselfishness, generosities, and magnanimities that he made his whole generation seem poor in these great qualities by comparison. Besides, he was in distress. His college had expelled him for writing an atheistical pamphlet and afflicting the reverend heads of the university with it, his rich father and grandfather had closed their purses against him, his friends were cold. Necessarily, Harriet fell in love with him; and so deeply, indeed, that there was no way for Shelley to save her from suicide but to marry her. He believed himself to blame for this state of things, so the marriage took place. He was pretty fairly in love with Harriet, although he loved Miss Hitchener better. He wrote and explained the case to Miss Hitchener after the wedding, and he could not have been franker or more naive and less stirred up about the circumstance if the matter in issue had been a commercial transaction involving thirty-five dollars.

Shelley was nineteen. He was not a youth, but a man. He had never had any youth. He was an erratic and fantastic child during eighteen years, then he stepped into manhood, as one steps over a door-sill. He was curiously mature at nineteen in his ability to do independent thinking on the deep questions of life and to arrive at sharply definite decisions regarding them, and stick to them--stick to them and stand by them at cost of bread, friendships, esteem, respect, and approbation.

In Defence of Harriet Shelley

For the sake of his opinions he was willing to sacrifice all these valuable things, and did sacrifice them; and went on doing it, too, when he could at any moment have made himself rich and supplied himself with friends and esteem by compromising with his father, at the moderate expense of throwing overboard one or two indifferent details of his cargo of principles.

He and Harriet eloped to Scotland and got married. They took lodgings in Edinburgh of a sort answerable to their purse, which was about empty, and there their life was a happy, one and grew daily more so. They had only themselves for company, but they needed no additions to it. They were as cozy and contented as birds in a nest. Harriet sang evenings or read aloud; also she studied and tried to improve her mind, her husband instructing her in Latin. She was very beautiful, she was modest, quiet, genuine, and, according to her husband's testimony, she had no fine lady airs or aspirations about her. In Matthew Arnold's judgment, she was "a pleasing figure."

The pair remained five weeks in Edinburgh, and then took lodgings in York, where Shelley's college mate, Hogg, lived. Shelley presently ran down to London, and Hogg took this opportunity to make love to the young wife. She repulsed him, and reported the fact to her husband when he got back. It seems a pity that Shelley did not copy this creditable conduct of hers some time or other when under temptation, so that we might have seen the author of his biography hang the miracle in the skies and squirt rainbows at it.

At the end of the first year of marriage--the most trying year for any young couple, for then the mutual failings are coming one by one to light, and the necessary adjustments are being made in pain and tribulation--Shelley was able to recognize that his marriage venture had been a safe one. As we have seen, his love for his wife had begun in a rather shallow way and with not much force, but now it was become deep and strong, which entitles his wife to a broad credit mark, one may admit. He addresses a long and loving poem to her, in which both passion and worship appear:

Exhibit A

"O thou
Whose dear love gleamed upon the gloomy path
Which this lone spirit travelled,
Wilt thou not turn
Those spirit-beaming eyes and look on me.
Until I be assured that Earth is Heaven

Mark Twain

And Heaven is Earth?
Harriet! let death all mortal ties dissolve,
But ours shall not be mortal."

Shelley also wrote a sonnet to her in August of this same year in celebration of her birthday:

Exhibit B

Ever as now with hove and Virtue's glow
May thy unwithering soul not cease to burn,
Still may thine heart with those pure thoughts o'erflow
Which force from mine such quick and warm return."

Was the girl of seventeen glad and proud and happy?

We may conjecture that she was.

That was the year 1812. Another year passed still happily, still successfully--a child was born in June, 1813, and in September, three months later, Shelley addresses a poem to this child, Ianthe, in which he points out just when the little creature is most particularly dear to him:

Exhibit C

"Dearest when most thy tender traits express
The image of thy mother's loveliness."

Up to this point the fabulist counsel for Shelley and prosecutor of his young wife has had easy sailing, but now his trouble begins, for Shelley is getting ready to make some unpleasant history for himself, and it will be necessary to put the blame of it on the wife.

Shelley had made the acquaintance of a charming gray-haired, young-hearted Mrs. Boinville, whose face "retained a certain youthful beauty"; she lived at Bracknell, and had a young daughter named Cornelia Turner, who was equipped with many fascinations. Apparently these people were sufficiently sentimental. Hogg says of Mrs. Boinville:

"The greater part of her associates were odious. I generally found there two or three sentimental young butchers, an eminently philosophical tinker, and several very unsophisticated medical practitioners or medical students, all of low origin and vulgar and offensive manners.

In Defence of Harriet Shelley

They sighed, turned up their eyes, retailed philosophy, such as it was," etc.

Shelley moved to Bracknell, July 27th (this is still 1813) purposely to be near this unwholesome prairie-dogs' nest. The fabulist says: "It was the entrance into a world more amiable and exquisite than he had yet known."

"In this acquaintance the attraction was mutual"--and presently it grew to be very mutual indeed, between Shelley and Cornelia Turner, when they got to studying the Italian poets together. Shelley, "responding like a tremulous instrument to every breath of passion or of sentiment," had his chance here. It took only four days for Cornelia's attractions to begin to dim Harriet's. Shelley arrived on the 27th of July; on the 31st he wrote a sonnet to Harriet in which "one detects already the little rift in the lover's lute which had seemed to be healed or never to have gaped at all when the later and happier sonnet to Ianthe was written"--in September, we remember:

Exhibit D

"EVENING. TO HARRIET

"O thou bright Sun! Beneath the dark blue line
Of western distance that sublime descendest,
And, gleaming lovelier as thy beams decline,
Thy million hues to every vapor lendest,
And over cobweb, lawn, and grove, and stream
Sheddest the liquid magic of thy light,
Till calm Earth, with the parting splendor bright,
Shows like the vision of a beauteous dream;
What gazer now with astronomic eye
Could coldly count the spots within thy sphere?
Such were thy lover, Harriet, could he fly
The thoughts of all that makes his passion dear,
And turning senseless from thy warm caress
Pick flaws in our close-woven happiness."

I cannot find the "rift"; still it may be there. What the poem seems to say is, that a person would be coldly ungrateful who could consent to count and consider little spots and flaws in such a warm, great, satisfying sun as Harriet is. It is a "little rift which had seemed to be healed, or never to have gaped at all." That is, "one detects" a little rift which perhaps had never existed. How does one do that? How does one see the invisible? It is the fabulist's secret; he knows how to detect what does not exist, he knows how to see what is not seeable; it is his gift, and he works it many a time to poor dead Harriet Shelley's deep damage.

"As yet, however, if there was a speck upon Shelley's happiness it was no more than a speck"--meaning the one which one detects where "it may never have gaped at all"--"nor had Harriet cause for discontent."

Shelley's Latin instructions to his wife had ceased. "From a teacher he had now become a pupil." Mrs. Boinville and her young married daughter Cornelia were teaching him Italian poetry; a fact which warns one to receive with some caution that other statement that Harriet had no "cause for discontent."

Shelley had stopped instructing Harriet in Latin, as before mentioned. The biographer thinks that the busy life in London some time back, and the intrusion of the baby, account for this. These were hindrances, but were there no others? He is always overlooking a detail here and there that might be valuable in helping us understand a situation. For instance, when a man has been hard at work at the Italian poets with a pretty woman, hour after hour, and responding like a tremulous instrument to every breath of passion or of sentiment in the meantime, that man is dog-tired when he gets home, and he can't teach his wife Latin; it would be unreasonable to expect it.

Up to this time we have submitted to having Mrs. Boinville pushed upon us as ostensibly concerned in these Italian lessons, but the biographer drops her now, of his own accord. Cornelia "perhaps" is sole teacher. Hogg says she was a prey to a kind of sweet melancholy, arising from causes purely imaginary; she required consolation, and found it in Petrarch. He also says, "Bysshe entered at once fully into her views and caught the soft infection, breathing the tenderest and sweetest melancholy, as every true poet ought."

Then the author of the book interlards a most stately and fine compliment to Cornelia, furnished by a man of approved judgment who knew her well "in later years." It is a very good compliment indeed, and she no doubt deserved it in her "later years," when she had for generations ceased to be sentimental and lackadaisical, and was no longer engaged in enchanting young husbands and sowing sorrow for young wives. But why is that compliment to that old gentlewoman intruded there? Is it to make the reader believe she was well-chosen and safe society for a young, sentimental husband? The biographer's device was not well planned. That old person was not present--it was her other self that was there, her young, sentimental, melancholy, warm-blooded self, in those early sweet times before antiquity had cooled her off and mossed her back.

"In choosing for friends such women as Mrs. Newton, Mrs. Boinville, and Cornelia Turner, Shelley gave good proof of his insight and discrimination." That is the fabulist's opinion--Harriet Shelley's is not reported.

Early in August, Shelley was in London trying to raise money. In September he wrote the poem to the baby, already quoted from. In the first week of October Shelley and family went to Warwick, then to Edinburgh, arriving there about the middle of the month.

"Harriet was happy." Why? The author furnishes a reason, but hides from us whether it is history or conjecture; it is because "the babe had borne the journey well." It has all the aspect of one of his artful devices-- flung in in his favorite casual way--the way he has when he wants to draw one's attention away from an obvious thing and amuse it with some trifle that is less obvious but more useful--in a history like this. The obvious thing is, that Harriet was happy because there was much territory between her husband and Cornelia Turner now; and because the perilous Italian lessons were taking a rest; and because, if there chanced to be any respondings like a tremulous instrument to every breath of passion or of sentiment in stock in these days, she might hope to get a share of them herself; and because, with her husband liberated, now, from the fetid fascinations of that sentimental retreat so pitilessly described by Hogg, who also dubbed it "Shelley's paradise" later, she might hope to persuade him to stay away from it permanently; and because she might also hope that his brain would cool, now, and his heart become healthy, and both brain and heart consider the situation and resolve that it would be a right and manly thing to stand by this girl-wife and her child and see that they were honorably dealt with, and cherished and protected and loved by the man that had promised these things, and so be made happy and kept so. And because, also--may we conjecture this? --we may hope for the privilege of taking up our cozy Latin lessons again, that used to be so pleasant, and brought us so near together-- so near, indeed, that often our heads touched, just as heads do over Italian lessons; and our hands met in casual and unintentional, but still most delicious and thrilling little contacts and momentary clasps, just as they inevitably do over Italian lessons. Suppose one should say to any young wife: "I find that your husband is poring over the Italian poets and being instructed in the beautiful Italian language by the lovely Cornelia Robinson"--would that cozy picture fail to rise before her mind? would its possibilities fail to suggest themselves to her? would there be a pang in her heart and a blush on her face? or, on the contrary, would the remark give her pleasure, make her joyous and gay? Why, one needs only to make the experiment--the result will not be uncertain.

However, we learn--by authority of deeply reasoned and searching conjecture--that the baby bore the journey well, and that that was why the young wife was happy. That accounts for two per cent. of the happiness, but it was not right to imply that it accounted for the other ninety-eight also.

Peacock, a scholar, poet, and friend of the Shelleys, was of their party when they went away. He used to laugh at the Boinville menagerie, and "was not a favorite." One of the Boinville group, writing to Hogg, said, "The Shelleys have made an addition to their party in the person of a cold scholar, who, I think, has neither taste nor feeling. This, Shelley will perceive sooner or later, for his warm nature craves sympathy." True, and Shelley will fight his way back there to get it--there will be no way to head him off.

Towards the end of November it was necessary for Shelley to pay a business visit to London, and he conceived the project of leaving Harriet and the baby in Edinburgh with Harriet's sister, Eliza Westbrook, a sensible, practical maiden lady about thirty years old, who had spent a great part of her time with the family since the marriage. She was an estimable woman, and Shelley had had reason to like her, and did like her; but along about this time his feeling towards her changed. Part of Shelley's plan, as he wrote Hogg, was to spend his London evenings with the Newtons--members of the Boinville Hysterical Society. But, alas, when he arrived early in December, that pleasant game was partially blocked, for Eliza and the family arrived with him. We are left destitute of conjectures at this point by the biographer, and it is my duty to supply one. I chance the conjecture that it was Eliza who interfered with that game. I think she tried to do what she could towards modifying the Boinville connection, in the interest of her young sister's peace and honor.

If it was she who blocked that game, she was not strong enough to block the next one. Before the month and year were out--no date given, let us call it

Christmas--Shelley and family were nested in a furnished house in Windsor, "at no great distance from the Boinvilles"--these decoys still residing at Bracknell.

What we need, now, is a misleading conjecture. We get it with characteristic promptness and depravity:

"But Prince Athanase found not the aged Zonoras, the friend of his boyhood, in any wanderings to Windsor. Dr. Lind had died a year since, and with his death Windsor must have lost, for Shelley, its chief attraction."

Still, not to mention Shelley's wife, there was Bracknell, at any rate. While Bracknell remains, all solace is not lost. Shelley is represented by this biographer as doing a great many careless things, but to my mind this hiring a furnished house for three months in order to be with a man who has been dead a year, is the carelessest of them all. One feels for him--that is but natural, and does us honor besides--yet one is vexed, for all that. He could have written and asked about the aged Zonoras before taking the house. He may not have had the address, but that is nothing--any postman would know the aged Zonoras; a dead postman would remember a name like that.

And yet, why throw a rag like this to us ravening wolves? Is it seriously supposable that we will stop to chew it and let our prey escape? No, we are getting to expect this kind of device, and to give it merely a sniff for certainty's sake and then walk around it and leave it lying. Shelley was not after the aged Zonoras; he was pointed for Cornelia and the Italian lessons, for his warm nature was craving sympathy.

CHAPTER II

The year 1813 is just ended now, and we step into 1814.

To recapitulate, how much of Cornelia's society has Shelley had, thus far? Portions of August and September, and four days of July. That is to say, he has had opportunity to enjoy it, more or less, during that brief period. Did he want some more of it? We must fall back upon history, and then go to conjecturing.

"In the early part of the year 1814, Shelley was a frequent visitor at Bracknell."
"Frequent" is a cautious word, in this author's mouth; the very cautiousness of it, the vagueness of it, provokes suspicion; it makes one suspect that this frequency was more frequent than the mere common everyday kinds of frequency which one is in the habit of averaging up with the unassuming term "frequent." I think so because they fixed up a bedroom for him in the Boinville house. One doesn't need a bedroom if one is only going to run over now and then in a disconnected way to respond like a tremulous instrument to every breath of passion or of sentiment and rub up one's Italian poetry a little.

The young wife was not invited, perhaps. If she was, she most certainly did not come, or she would have straightened the room up; the most ignorant of us knows that a wife would not endure a room in the condition in which Hogg found this one when he occupied it one night. Shelley was away-- why, nobody can divine. Clothes were scattered about, there were books on every side: "Wherever a book could be laid was an open book turned down on its face to keep its place." It seems plain that the wife was not invited. No, not that; I think she was invited, but said to herself that she could not bear to go there and see another young woman touching heads with her husband over an Italian book and making thrilling hand-contacts with him accidentally.

As remarked, he was a frequent visitor there, "where he found an easeful resting-place in the house of Mrs. Boinville--the white-haired Maimuna-- and of her daughter, Mrs. Turner." The aged Zonoras was deceased, but the white-haired Maimuna was still on deck, as we see. "Three charming ladies entertained the mocker (Hogg) with cups of tea, late hours, Wieland's Agathon, sighs and smiles, and the celestial manna of refined sentiment."

"Such," says Hogg, "were the delights of Shelley's paradise in Bracknell."

The white-haired Maimuna presently writes to Hogg:

"I will not have you despise home-spun pleasures. Shelley is making a trial of them with us--"
A trial of them. It may be called that. It was March 11, and he had been in the house a month. She continues:

Shelley *"likes then so well that he is resolved to leave off rambling--"*
But he has already left it off. He has been there a month.

"And begin a course of them himself."
But he has already begun it. He has been at it a month. He likes it so well that he has forgotten all about his wife, as a letter of his reveals.

"Seriously, I think his mind and body want rest."
Yet he has been resting both for a month, with Italian, and tea, and manna of sentiment, and late hours, and every restful thing a young husband could need for the refreshment of weary limbs and a sore conscience, and a nagging sense of shabbiness and treachery.

"His journeys after what he has never found have racked his purse and his tranquillity. He is resolved to take a little care of the former, in pity to the latter, which I applaud, and shall second with all, my might."
But she does not say whether the young wife, a stranger and lonely yonder, wants another woman and her daughter Cornelia to be lavishing so much inflamed interest on her husband or not. That young wife is always silent-- we are never allowed to hear from her. She must have opinions about such things, she cannot be indifferent, she must be approving or disapproving, surely she would speak if she were allowed--even to-day and from her grave

she would, if she could, I think--but we get only the other side, they keep her silent always.

"He has deeply interested us. In the course of your intimacy he must have made you feel what we now feel for him. He is seeking a house close to us--"

Ah! he is not close enough yet, it seems--"and if he succeeds we shall have an additional motive to induce you to come among us in the summer."

The reader would puzzle a long time and not guess the biographer's comment upon the above letter. It is this:

"These sound like words of s considerate and judicious friend."
That is what he thinks. That is, it is what he thinks he thinks. No, that is not quite it: it is what he thinks he can stupefy a particularly and unspeakably dull reader into thinking it is what he thinks. He makes that comment with the knowledge that Shelley is in love with this woman's daughter, and that it is because of the fascinations of these two that Shelley has deserted his wife--for this month, considering all the circumstances, and his new passion, and his employment of the time, amounted to desertion; that is its rightful name. We cannot know how the wife regarded it and felt about it; but if she could have read the letter which Shelley was writing to Hogg four or five days later, we could guess her thought and how she felt. Hear him:

*"I have been staying with Mrs. Boinville for the last month;
I have escaped, in the society of all that philosophy and
friendship combine, from the dismaying solitude of myself."*
It is fair to conjecture that he was feeling ashamed.

*"They have revived in my heart the expiring flame of life.
I have felt myself translated to a paradise which has nothing of mortality but its
transitoriness; my heart sickens at the view of that necessity which will quickly
divide me from the delightful tranquillity of this happy home--for it has become my
home.
"Eliza is still with us--not here!--but will be with me when the infinite malice of
destiny forces me to depart."*

Eliza is she who blocked that game--the game in London--the one where we were purposing to dine every night with one of the "three charming ladies" who fed tea and manna and late hours to Hogg at Bracknell.

In Defence of Harriet Shelley

Shelley could send Eliza away, of course; could have cleared her out long ago if so minded, just as he had previously done with a predecessor of hers whom he had first worshipped and then turned against; but perhaps she was useful there as a thin excuse for staying away himself.

"I am now but little inclined to contest this point. I certainly hate her with all my heart and soul . . . .
"It is a sight which awakens an inexpressible sensation of disgust and horror, to see her caress my poor little Ianthe, in whom I may hereafter find the consolation of sympathy. I sometimes feel faint with the fatigue of checking the overflowings of my unbounded abhorrence for this miserable wretch. But she is no more than a blind and loathsome worm ,that cannot see to sting.

"I have begun to learn Italian again . . . . Cornelia assists me in this language. Did I not once tell you that I thought her cold and reserved? She is the reverse of this, as she is the reverse of everything bad. She inherits all the divinity of her mother . . . . I have sometimes forgotten that I am not an inmate of this delightful home--that a time will come which will cast me again into the boundless ocean of abhorred society.
"I have written nothing but one stanza, which has no meaning, and that I have only written in thought:

"Thy dewy looks sink in my breast;
Thy gentle words stir poison there;
Thou hast disturbed the only rest
That was the portion of despair.
Subdued to duty's hard control,
I could have borne my wayward lot:
The chains that bind this rained soul
Had cankered then, but crushed it not.

"This is the vision of a delirious and distempered dream, which passes away at the cold clear light of morning. Its surpassing excellence and exquisite perfections have no more reality than the color of an autumnal sunset."

Then it did not refer to his wife. That is plain; otherwise he would have said so. It is well that he explained that it has no meaning, for if he had not done that, the previous soft references to Cornelia and the way he has come to feel about her now would make us think she was the person who had inspired it while teaching him how to read the warm and ruddy Italian poets during a month.

The biography observes that portions of this letter "read like the tired moaning of a wounded creature." Guesses at the nature of the wound are permissible; we will hazard one.

Read by the light of Shelley's previous history, his letter seems to be the cry of a tortured conscience. Until this time it was a conscience that had never felt a pang or known a smirch. It was the conscience of one who, until this time, had never done a dishonorable thing, or an ungenerous, or cruel, or treacherous thing, but was now doing all of these, and was keenly aware of it. Up to this time Shelley had been master of his nature, and it was a nature which was as beautiful and as nearly perfect as any merely human nature may be. But he was drunk now, with a debasing passion, and was not himself. There is nothing in his previous history that is in character with the Shelley of this letter. He had done boyish things, foolish things, even crazy things, but never a thing to be ashamed of. He had done things which one might laugh at, but the privilege of laughing was limited always to the thing itself; you could not laugh at the motive back of it--that was high, that was noble. His most fantastic and quixotic acts had a purpose back of them which made them fine, often great, and made the rising laugh seem profanation and quenched it; quenched it, and changed the impulse to homage.

Up to this time he had been loyalty itself, where his obligations lay-- treachery was new to him; he had never done an ignoble thing--baseness was new to him; he had never done an unkind thing that also was new to him.

This was the author of that letter, this was the man who had deserted his young wife and was lamenting, because he must leave another woman's house which had become a "home" to him, and go away. Is he lamenting mainly because he must go back to his wife and child? No, the lament is mainly for what he is to leave behind him. The physical comforts of the house? No, in his life he had never attached importance to such things. Then the thing which he grieves to leave is narrowed down to a person--to the person whose "dewy looks" had sunk into his breast, and whose seducing words had "stirred poison there."

He was ashamed of himself, his conscience was upbraiding him. He was the slave of a degrading love; he was drunk with his passion, the real Shelley was in temporary eclipse. This is the verdict which his previous history must certainly deliver upon this episode, I think.

One must be allowed to assist himself with conjectures like these when trying to find his way through a literary swamp which has so many misleading finger-boards up as this book is furnished with.

We have now arrived at a part of the swamp where the difficulties and perplexities are going to be greater than any we have yet met with-- where, indeed, the finger-boards are multitudinous, and the most of them pointing diligently in the wrong direction. We are to be told by the biography why Shelley deserted his wife and child and took up with Cornelia Turner and Italian. It was not on account of Cornelia's sighs and sentimentalities and tea and manna and late hours and soft and sweet and industrious enticements; no, it was because "his happiness in his home had been wounded and bruised almost to death."

It had been wounded and bruised almost to death in this way:

1st. Harriet persuaded him to set up a carriage.

2d. After the intrusion of the baby, Harriet stopped reading aloud and studying.

3d. Harriet's walks with Hogg "commonly conducted us to some fashionable bonnet-shop."

4th. Harriet hired a wet-nurse.

5th. When an operation was being performed upon the baby, "Harriet stood by, narrowly observing all that was done, but, to the astonishment of the operator, betraying not the smallest sign of emotion."

6th. Eliza Westbrook, sister-in-law, was still of the household.

The evidence against Harriet Shelley is all in; there is no more. Upon these six counts she stands indicted of the crime of driving her husband into that sty at Bracknell; and this crime, by these helps, the biographical prosecuting attorney has set himself the task of proving upon her.

Does the biographer call himself the attorney for the prosecution? No, only to himself, privately; publicly he is the passionless, disinterested, impartial judge on the bench. He holds up his judicial scales before the world, that all may see; and it all tries to look so fair that a blind person would sometimes fail to see him slip the false weights in.

Shelley's happiness in his home had been wounded and bruised almost to death, first, because Harriet had persuaded him to set up a carriage. I cannot discover that any evidence is offered that she asked him to set up a carriage. Still, if she did, was it a heavy offence? Was it unique? Other young wives had committed it before, others have committed it since. Shelley had dearly loved her in those London days; possibly he set up the carriage gladly to please her; affectionate young husbands do such things. When Shelley ran away with another girl, by-and-by, this girl persuaded him to pour the price of many carriages and many horses down the bottomless well of her father's debts, but this impartial judge finds no fault with that. Once she appeals to Shelley to raise money-- necessarily by borrowing, there was no other way-- to pay her father's debts with at a time when Shelley was in danger of being arrested and imprisoned for his own debts; yet the good judge finds no fault with her even for this.

First and last, Shelley emptied into that rapacious mendicant's lap a sum which cost him--for he borrowed it at ruinous rates--from eighty to one hundred thousand dollars. But it was Mary Godwin's papa, the supplications were often sent through Mary, the good judge is Mary's strenuous friend, so Mary gets no censures. On the Continent Mary rode in her private carriage, built, as Shelley boasts, "by one of the best makers in Bond Street, "yet the good judge makes not even a passing comment on this iniquity. Let us throw out Count No. 1 against Harriet Shelley as being far-fetched, and frivolous.

Shelley's happiness in his home had been wounded and bruised almost to death, secondly, because Harriet's studies "had dwindled away to nothing, Bysshe had ceased to express any interest in them." At what time was this? It was when Harriet "had fully recovered from the fatigue of her first effort of maternity,. . . and was now in full force, vigor, and effect." Very well, the baby was born two days before the close of June. It took the mother a month to get back her full force, vigor, and effect; this brings us to July 27th and the deadly Cornelia. If a wife of eighteen is studying with her husband and he gets smitten with another woman, isn't he likely to lose interest in his wife's studies for that reason, and is not his wife's interest in her studies likely to languish for the same reason? Would not the mere sight of those books of hers sharpen the pain that is in her heart? This sudden breaking down of a mutual intellectual interest of two years' standing is coincident with Shelley's re-encounter with Cornelia; and we are allowed to gather from that time forth for nearly two months he did all his studying in that person's society. We feel at liberty to rule out Count No. 2 from the indictment against Harriet.

Shelley's happiness in his home had been wounded and bruised almost to death, thirdly, because Harriet's walks with Hogg commonly led to some fashionable bonnet-shop. I offer no palliation; I only ask why the dispassionate, impartial judge did not offer one himself--merely, I mean, to offset his leniency in a similar case or two where the girl who ran away with Harriet's husband was the shopper. There are several occasions where she interested herself with shopping--among them being walks which ended at the bonnet-shop--yet in none of these cases does she get a word of blame from the good judge, while in one of them he covers the deed with a justifying remark, she doing the shopping that time to find easement for her mind, her child having died.

Shelley's happiness in his home had been wounded and bruised almost to death, fourthly, by the introduction there of a wet-nurse. The wet-nurse was introduced at the time of the Edinburgh sojourn, immediately after Shelley had been enjoying the two months of study with Cornelia which broke up his wife's studies and destroyed his personal interest in them. Why, by this time, nothing that Shelley's wife could do would have been satisfactory to him, for he was in love with another woman, and was never going to be contented again until he got back to her. If he had been still in love with his wife it is not easily conceivable that he would care much who nursed the baby, provided the baby was well nursed. Harriet's jealousy was assuredly voicing itself now, Shelley's conscience was assuredly nagging him, pestering him, persecuting him. Shelley needed excuses for his altered attitude towards his wife; Providence pitied him and sent the wet-nurse. If Providence had sent him a cotton doughnut it would have answered just as well; all he wanted was something to find fault with.

Shelley's happiness in his home had been wounded and bruised almost to death, fifthly, because Harriet narrowly watched a surgical operation which was being performed upon her child, and, "to the astonishment of the operator," who was watching Harriet instead of attending to his operation, she betrayed "not the smallest sign of emotion." The author of this biography was not ashamed to set down that exultant slander. He was apparently not aware that it was a small business to bring into his court a witness whose name he does not know, and whose character and veracity there is none to vouch for, and allow him to strike this blow at the mother-heart of this friendless girl. The biographer says, "We may not infer from this that Harriet did not feel"--why put it in, then?-- "but we learn that those about her could believe her to be hard and insensible." Who were those who were about her? Her husband? He hated her now, because he was in love elsewhere. Her sister? Of course that is not charged. Peacock? Peacock does not testify. The wet-nurse? She does not testify. If any others were there we have no mention of them. "Those about her" are reduced to one person--her husband. Who reports the circumstance? It is Hogg. Perhaps he was there-- we do not know. But if he was, he still got his information at second-hand, as it was the operator who noticed Harriet's lack of emotion, not himself. Hogg is not given to saying kind things when Harriet is his subject. He may have said them the time that he tried to tempt her to soil her honor, but after that he mentions her usually with a sneer. "Among those who were about her" was one witness well equipped to silence all tongues, abolish all doubts, set our minds at rest; one witness, not called, and not callable, whose evidence, if we could but get it, would outweigh the oaths of whole battalions of hostile Hoggs and nameless surgeons--the baby. I wish we had the baby's testimony; and yet if we had it it would not do us any good--a furtive conjecture, a sly insinuation, a pious "if" or two, would be smuggled in, here and there, with a solemn air of judicial investigation, and its positiveness would wilt into dubiety.

The biographer says of Harriet, "If words of tender affection and motherly pride proved the reality of love, then undoubtedly she loved her firstborn child." That is, if mere empty words can prove it, it stands proved--and in this way, without committing himself, he gives the reader a chance to infer that there isn't any extant evidence but words, and that he doesn't take much stock in them. How seldom he shows his hand! He is always lurking behind a non-committal "if" or something of that kind; always gliding and dodging around, distributing colorless poison here and there and everywhere, but always leaving himself in a position to say that his language will be found innocuous if taken to pieces and examined. He clearly exhibits a steady and never-relaxing purpose to make Harriet the scapegoat for her husband's first great sin--but it is in the general view that this is revealed, not in the details.

His insidious literature is like blue water; you know what it is that makes it blue, but you cannot produce and verify any detail of the cloud of microscopic dust in it that does it. Your adversary can dip up a glassful and show you that it is pure white and you cannot deny it; and he can dip the lake dry, glass by glass, and show that every glassful is white, and prove it to any one's eye--and yet that lake was blue and you can swear it. This book is blue--with slander in solution.

Let the reader examine, for example, the paragraph of comment which immediately follows the letter containing Shelley's self-exposure which we have been considering. This is it. One should inspect the individual sentences as they go by, then pass them in procession and review the cake-walk as a whole:

> *"Shelley's happiness in his home, as is evident from this pathetic letter, had been fatally stricken; it is evident, also, that he knew where duty lay; he felt that his part was to take up his burden, silently and sorrowfully, and to bear it henceforth with the quietness of despair. But we can perceive that he scarcely possessed the strength and fortitude needful for success in such an attempt. And clearly Shelley himself was aware how perilous it was to accept that respite of blissful ease which he enjoyed in the Boinville household; for gentle voices and dewy looks and words of sympathy could not fail to remind him of an ideal of tranquillity or of joy which could never be his, and which he must henceforth sternly exclude from his imagination."*

That paragraph commits the author in no way. Taken sentence by sentence it asserts nothing against anybody or in favor of anybody, pleads for nobody, accuses nobody. Taken detail by detail, it is as innocent as moonshine. And yet, taken as a whole, it is a design against the reader; its intent is to remove the feeling which the letter must leave with him if let alone, and put a different one in its place--to remove a feeling justified by the letter and substitute one not justified by it. The letter itself gives you no uncertain picture--no lecturer is needed to stand by with a stick and point out its details and let on to explain what they mean. The picture is the very clear and remorsefully faithful picture of a fallen and fettered angel who is ashamed of himself; an angel who beats his soiled wings and cries, who complains to the woman who enticed him that he could have borne his wayward lot, he could have stood by his duty if it had not been for her beguilements; an angel who rails at the "boundless ocean of abhorred society," and rages at his poor judicious sister-in-law. If there is any dignity about this spectacle it will escape most people.

Yet when the paragraph of comment is taken as a whole, the picture is full of dignity and pathos; we have before us a blameless and noble spirit stricken to the earth by malign powers, but not conquered; tempted, but grandly putting the temptation away; enmeshed by subtle coils, but sternly resolved to rend them and march forth victorious, at any peril of life or limb. Curtain--slow music.

Was it the purpose of the paragraph to take the bad taste of Shelley's letter out of the reader's mouth? If that was not it, good ink was wasted; without that, it has no relevancy--the multiplication table would have padded the space as rationally.

We have inspected the six reasons which we are asked to believe drove a man of conspicuous patience, honor, justice, fairness, kindliness, and iron firmness, resolution, and steadfastness, from the wife whom he loved and who loved him, to a refuge in the mephitic paradise of Bracknell. These are six infinitely little reasons; but there were six colossal ones, and these the counsel for the destruction of Harriet Shelley persists in not considering very important.

Moreover, the colossal six preceded the little six and had done the mischief before they were born. Let us double-column the twelve; then we shall see at a glance that each little reason is in turn answered by a retorting reason of a size to overshadow it and make it insignificant:

1. Harriet sets up carriage. 1. CORNELIA TURNER.

2. Harriet stops studying. 2. CORNELIA TURNER.

3. Harriet goes to bonnet-shop. 3. CORNELIA TURNER.

4. Harriet takes a wet-nurse. 4. CORNELIA TURNER.

5. Harriet has too much nerve. 5. CORNELIA TURNER.

6. Detested sister-in-law.fi. 6. CORNELIA TURNER.

As soon as we comprehend that Cornelia Turner and the Italian lessons happened before the little six had been discovered to be grievances, we understand why Shelley's happiness in his home had been wounded and bruised almost to death, and no one can persuade us into laying it on Harriet.

Shelley and Cornelia are the responsible persons, and we cannot in honor and decency allow the cruelties which they practised upon the unoffending wife to be pushed aside in order to give us a chance to waste time and tears over six sentimental justifications of an offence which the six can't justify, nor even respectably assist in justifying.

Six? There were seven; but in charity to the biographer the seventh ought not to be exposed. Still, he hung it out himself, and not only hung it out, but thought it was a good point in Shelley's favor. For two years Shelley found sympathy and intellectual food and all that at home; there was enough for spiritual and mental support, but not enough for luxury; and so, at the end of the contented two years, this latter detail justifies him in going bag and baggage over to Cornelia Turner and supplying the rest of his need in the way of surplus sympathy and intellectual pie unlawfully. By the same reasoning a man in merely comfortable circumstances may rob a bank without sin.

CHAPTER III

It is 1814, it is the 16th of March, Shelley has, written his letter, he has been in the Boinville paradise a month, his deserted wife is in her husbandless home. Mischief had been wrought. It is the biographer who concedes this. We greatly need some light on Harriet's side of the case now; we need to know how she enjoyed the month, but there is no way to inform ourselves; there seems to be a strange absence of documents and letters and diaries on that side. Shelley kept a diary, the approaching Mary Godwin kept a diary, her father kept one, her half-sister by marriage, adoption, and the dispensation of God kept one, and the entire tribe and all its friends wrote and received letters, and the letters were kept and are producible when this biography needs them; but there are only three or four scraps of Harriet's writing, and no diary. Harriet wrote plenty of letters to her husband--nobody knows where they are, I suppose; she wrote plenty of letters to other people--apparently they have disappeared, too. Peacock says she wrote good letters, but apparently interested people had sagacity enough to mislay them in time. After all her industry she went down into her grave and lies silent there-- silent, when she has so much need to speak. We can only wonder at this mystery, not account for it.

No, there is no way of finding out what Harriet's state of feeling was during the month that Shelley was disporting himself in the Bracknell paradise. We have to fall back upon conjecture, as our fabulist does when he has nothing more substantial to work with. Then we easily conjecture that as the days dragged by Harriet's heart grew heavier and heavier under its two burdens-- shame and resentment: the shame of being pointed at and gossiped about as a deserted wife, and resentment against the woman who had beguiled her husband from her and now kept him in a disreputable captivity. Deserted wives--deserted whether for cause or without cause--find small charity among the virtuous and the discreet. We conjecture that one after another the neighbors ceased to call; that one after another they got to being "engaged" when Harriet called; that finally they one after the other cut her dead on the street; that after that she stayed in the house daytimes, and brooded over her sorrows, and nighttimes did the same, there being nothing else to do with the heavy hours and the silence and solitude and the dreary intervals which sleep should have charitably bridged, but didn't.

Yes, mischief had been wrought. The biographer arrives at this conclusion, and it is a most just one. Then, just as you begin to half hope he is going to discover the cause of it and launch hot bolts of wrath at the guilty manufacturers of it, you have to turn away disappointed. You are disappointed, and you sigh. This is what he says --the italics ["] are mine:

"However the mischief may have been wrought--'and at this day no one can wish to heap blame an any buried head'--"

So it is poor Harriet, after all. Stern justice must take its course-- justice tempered with delicacy, justice tempered with compassion, justice that pities a forlorn dead girl and refuses to strike her. Except in the back. Will not be ignoble and say the harsh thing, but only insinuate it. Stern justice knows about the carriage and the wet-nurse and the bonnet-shop and the other dark things that caused this sad mischief, and may not, must not blink them; so it delivers judgment where judgment belongs, but softens the blow by not seeming to deliver judgment at all. To resume--the italics are mine:

"However the mischief may have been wrought--and at this day no one can wish to heap blame on any buried head--'it is certain that some cause or causes of deep division between Shelley and his wife were in operation during the early part of the year 1814'."

This shows penetration. No deduction could be more accurate than this. There were indeed some causes of deep division. But next comes another disappointing sentence:

"To guess at the precise nature of these cafes, in the absence of definite statement, were useless."

Why, he has already been guessing at them for several pages, and we have been trying to outguess him, and now all of a sudden he is tired of it and won't play any more. It is not quite fair to us. However, he will get over this by-and-by, when Shelley commits his next indiscretion and has to be guessed out of it at Harriet's expense.

"We may rest content with Shelley's own words"--in a Chancery paper drawn up by him three years later. They were these: "Delicacy forbids me to say more than that we were disunited by incurable dissensions."

As for me, I do not quite see why we should rest content with anything of the sort. It is not a very definite statement. It does not necessarily mean anything more than that he did not wish to go into the tedious details of those family quarrels. Delicacy could quite properly excuse him from saying, "I was in love with Cornelia all that time; my wife kept crying and worrying about it and upbraiding me and begging me to cut myself free from a connection which was wronging her and disgracing us both; and I being stung by these reproaches retorted with fierce and bitter speeches--for it is my nature to do that when I am stirred, especially if the target of them is a person whom I had greatly loved and respected before, as witness my various attitudes towards Miss Hitchener, the Gisbornes, Harriet's sister, and others--and finally I did not improve this state of things when I deserted my wife and spent a whole month with the woman who had infatuated me."

No, he could not go into those details, and we excuse him; but, nevertheless, we do not rest content with this bland proposition to puff away that whole long disreputable episode with a single mean, meaningless remark of Shelley's.

We do admit that "it is certain that some cause or causes of deep division were in operation." We would admit it just the same if the grammar of the statement were as straight as a string, for we drift into pretty indifferent grammar ourselves when we are absorbed in historical work; but we have to decline to admit that we cannot guess those cause or causes.

But guessing is not really necessary. There is evidence attainable-- evidence from the batch discredited by the biographer and set out at the back door in his appendix-basket; and yet a court of law would think twice before throwing it out, whereas it would be a hardy person who would venture to offer in such a place a good part of the material which is placed before the readers of this book as "evidence," and so treated by this daring biographer. Among some letters (in the appendix-basket) from Mrs. Godwin, detailing the Godwinian share in the Shelleyan events of 1814, she tells how Harriet

Shelley came to her and her husband, agitated and weeping, to implore them to forbid Shelley the house, and prevent his seeing Mary Godwin.

"She related that last November he had fallen in love with Mrs. Turner and paid her such marked attentions Mr. Turner, the husband, had carried off his wife to Devonshire."

The biographer finds a technical fault in this; "the Shelleys were in Edinburgh in November." What of that? The woman is recalling a conversation which is more than two months old; besides, she was probably more intent upon the central and important fact of it than upon its unimportant date. Harriet's quoted statement has some sense in it; for that reason, if for no other, it ought to have been put in the body of the book. Still, that would not have answered; even the biographer's enemy could not be cruel enough to ask him to let this real grievance, this compact and substantial and picturesque figure, this rawhead-and- bloody-bones, come striding in there among those pale shams, those rickety spectres labeled WET-NURSE, BONNET-SHOP, and so on--no, the father of all malice could not ask the biographer to expose his pathetic goblins to a competition like that.

The fabulist finds fault with the statement because it has a technical error in it; and he does this at the moment that he is furnishing us an error himself, and of a graver sort. He says:

"If Turner carried off his wife to Devonshire he brought her back and Shelley was staying with her and her mother on terms of cordial intimacy in March, 1814."

We accept the "cordial intimacy"--it was the very thing Harriet was complaining of--but there is nothing to show that it was Turner who brought his wife back. The statement is thrown in as if it were not only true, but was proof that Turner was not uneasy. Turner's movements are proof of nothing. Nothing but a statement from Turner's mouth would have any value here, and he made none.

Six days after writing his letter Shelley and his wife were together again for a moment--to get remarried according to the rites of the English Church.

Within three weeks the new husband and wife were apart again, and the former was back in his odorous paradise. This time it is the wife who does the deserting. She finds Cornelia too strong for her, probably. At any rate, she goes away with her baby and sister, and we have a playful fling at her from good Mrs. Boinville, the "mysterious spinner Maimuna"; she whose "face was as a damsel's face, and yet her hair was gray"; she of whom the biographer has said, "Shelley was indeed caught in an almost invisible thread spun around him, but unconsciously, by this subtle and benignant enchantress." The subtle and benignant enchantress writes to Hogg, April 18: "Shelley is again a widower; his beauteous half went to town on Thursday."

Then Shelley writes a poem--a chant of grief over the hard fate which obliges him now to leave his paradise and take up with his wife again. It seems to intimate that the paradise is cooling towards him; that he is warned off by acclamation; that he must not even venture to tempt with one last tear his friend Cornelia's ungentle mood, for her eye is glazed and cold and dares not entreat her lover to stay:

Exhibit E

"Pause not! the time is past! Every voice cries 'Away!'
Tempt not with one last tear thy friend's ungentle mood;
Thy lover's eye, so glazed and cold, dares not entreat thy stay: Duty and dereliction
guide thee back to solitude."

Back to the solitude of his now empty home, that is!

"Away! away! to thy sad and silent home;
Pour bitter tears on its desolated hearth."
But he will have rest in the grave by-and-by. Until that time comes, the charms of
Bracknell will remain in his memory, along with Mrs. Boinville's voice and
Cornelia Turner's smile:
"Thou in the grave shalt rest--yet, till the phantoms flee
Which that house and hearth and garden made dear to thee ere while, Thy
remembrance and repentance and deep musings are not free From the music of two
voices and the light of one sweet smile."

We cannot wonder that Harriet could not stand it. Any of us would have left. We would not even stay with a cat that was in this condition. Even the Boinvilles could not endure it; and so, as we have seen, they gave this one notice.

"Early in May, Shelley was in London. He did not yet despair
of reconciliation with Harriet, nor had he ceased to love her."

In Defence of Harriet Shelley

Shelley's poems are a good deal of trouble to his biographer. They are constantly inserted as "evidence," and they make much confusion. As soon as one of them has proved one thing, another one follows and proves quite a different thing. The poem just quoted shows that he was in love with Cornelia, but a month later he is in love with Harriet again, and there is a poem to prove it.

"In this piteous appeal Shelley declares that he has now no grief but one--the grief of having known and lost his wife's love."
Exhibit F

> *"Thy look of love has power to calm*
> *The stormiest passion of my soul."*

But without doubt she had been reserving her looks of love a good part of the time for ten months, now--ever since he began to lavish his own on Cornelia Turner at the end of the previous July. He does really seem to have already forgotten Cornelia's merits in one brief month, for he eulogizes Harriet in a way which rules all competition out:

> *"Thou only virtuous, gentle, kind,*
> *Amid a world of hate."*

He complains of her hardness, and begs her to make the concession of a "slight endurance"--of his waywardness, perhaps--for the sake of "a fellow-being's lasting weal." But the main force of his appeal is in his closing stanza, and is strongly worded:

> *"O tract for once no erring guide!*
> *Bid the remorseless feeling flee;*
> *'Tis malice, 'tis revenge, 'tis pride,*
> *'Tis anything but thee;*
> *I deign a nobler pride to prove,*
> *And pity if thou canst not love."*

This is in May--apparently towards the end of it. Harriet and Shelley were corresponding all the time. Harriet got the poem--a copy exists in her own handwriting; she being the only gentle and kind person amid a world of hate, according to Shelley's own testimony in the poem, we are permitted to think that the daily letters would presently have melted that kind and gentle heart and brought about the reconciliation, if there had been time but there wasn't; for in a very few days--in fact, before the 8th of June--Shelley was in love with another woman.

And so--perhaps while Harriet was walking the floor nights, trying to get her poem by heart--her husband was doing a fresh one--for the other girl --Mary Wollstonecraft Godwin--with sentiments like these in it:

Exhibit G

> To spend years thus and be rewarded,
> As thou, sweet love, requited me
> When none were near.
> thy lips did meet
> Mine tremblingly;

" Gentle and good and mild thou art, Nor can I live if thou appear Aught but thyself." . . .

And so on. "Before the close of June it was known and felt by Mary and Shelley that each was inexpressibly dear to the other." Yes, Shelley had found this child of sixteen to his liking, and had wooed and won her in the graveyard. But that is nothing; it was better than wooing her in her nursery, at any rate, where it might have disturbed the other children.

However, she was a child in years only. From the day that she set her masculine grip on Shelley he was to frisk no more. If she had occupied the only kind and gentle Harriet's place in March it would have been a thrilling spectacle to see her invade the Boinville rookery and read the riot act. That holiday of Shelley's would have been of short duration, and Cornelia's hair would have been as gray as her mother's when the services were over.

Hogg went to the Godwin residence in Skinner Street with Shelley on that 8th of June. They passed through Godwin's little debt-factory of a book-shop and went up-stairs hunting for the proprietor. Nobody there. Shelley strode about the room impatiently, making its crazy floor quake under him. Then a door "was partially and softly opened. A thrilling voice called 'Shelley!' A thrilling voice answered, 'Mary!' And he darted out of the room like an arrow from the bow of the far-shooting King. A very young female, fair and fair-haired, pale, indeed, and with a piercing look, wearing a frock of tartan, an unusual dress in London at that time, had called him out of the room."

In Defence of Harriet Shelley

This is Mary Godwin, as described by Hogg. The thrill of the voices shows that the love of Shelley and Mary was already upward of a fortnight old; therefore it had been born within the month of May--born while Harriet was still trying to get her poem by heart, we think. I must not be asked how I know so much about that thrill; it is my secret. The biographer and I have private ways of finding out things when it is necessary to find them out and the customary methods fail.

Shelley left London that day, and was gone ten days. The biographer conjectures that he spent this interval with Harriet in Bath. It would be just like him. To the end of his days he liked to be in love with two women at once. He was more in love with Miss Hitchener when he married Harriet than he was with Harriet, and told the lady so with simple and unostentatious candor. He was more in love with Cornelia than he was with Harriet in the end of 1813 and the beginning of 1814, yet he supplied both of them with love poems of an equal temperature meantime; he loved Mary and Harriet in June, and while getting ready to run off with the one, it is conjectured that he put in his odd time trying to get reconciled to the other; by-and-by, while still in love with Mary, he will make love to her half-sister by marriage, adoption, and the visitation of God, through the medium of clandestine letters, and she will answer with letters that are for no eye but his own.

When Shelley encountered Mary Godwin he was looking around for another paradise. He had, tastes of his own, and there were features about the Godwin establishment that strongly recommended it. Godwin was an advanced thinker and an able writer. One of his romances is still read, but his philosophical works, once so esteemed, are out of vogue now; their authority was already declining when Shelley made his acquaintance --that is, it was declining with the public, but not with Shelley. They had been his moral and political Bible, and they were that yet. Shelley the infidel would himself have claimed to be less a work of God than a work of Godwin. Godwin's philosophies had formed his mind and interwoven themselves into it and become a part of its texture; he regarded himself as Godwin's spiritual son. Godwin was not without self-appreciation; indeed, it may be conjectured that from his point of view the last syllable of his name was surplusage. He lived serene in his lofty world of philosophy, far above the mean interests that absorbed smaller men, and only came down to the ground at intervals to pass the hat for alms to pay his debts with, and insult the man that relieved him. Several of his principles were out of the ordinary. For example, he was opposed to marriage. He was not aware that his preachings from this text were but theory and wind; he supposed he was in earnest in imploring people to live together without marrying, until Shelley furnished him a working model of his scheme and a practical example to analyze, by applying the principle in his own family; the matter took a different and surprising aspect then. The late Matthew Arnold said that the main defect in Shelley's make-up was that he was destitute of the sense of humor. This episode must have escaped Mr. Arnold's attention.

But we have said enough about the head of the new paradise. Mrs. Godwin is described as being in several ways a terror; and even when her soul was in repose she wore green spectacles. But I suspect that her main unattractiveness was born of the fact that she wrote the letters that are out in the appendix-basket in the back yard--letters which are an outrage and wholly untrustworthy, for they say some kind things about poor Harriet and tell some disagreeable truths about her husband; and these things make the fabulist grit his teeth a good deal.

Next we have Fanny Godwin--a Godwin by courtesy only; she was Mrs. Godwin's natural daughter by a former friend. She was a sweet and winning girl, but she presently wearied of the Godwin paradise, and poisoned herself.

Last in the list is Jane (or Claire, as she preferred to call herself) Clairmont, daughter of Mrs. Godwin by a former marriage. She was very young and pretty and accommodating, and always ready to do what she could to make things pleasant. After Shelley ran off with her part-sister Mary, she became the guest of the pair, and contributed a natural child to their nursery-- Allegra. Lord Byron was the father.

We have named the several members and advantages of the new paradise in Skinner Street, with its crazy book-shop underneath. Shelley was all right now, this was a better place than the other; more variety anyway, and more different kinds of fragrance. One could turn out poetry here without any trouble at all.

The way the new love-match came about was this:

Shelley told Mary all his aggravations and sorrows and griefs, and about the wet-nurse and the bonnet shop and the surgeon and the carriage, and the sister-in-law that blocked the London game, and about Cornelia and her mamma, and how they had turned him out of the house after making so much of him; and how he had deserted Harriet and then Harriet had deserted him, and how the reconciliation was working along and Harriet getting her poem by heart; and still he was not happy, and Mary pitied him, for she had had trouble herself. But I am not satisfied with this. It reads too much like statistics. It lacks smoothness and grace, and is too earthy and business-like. It has the sordid look of a trades-union procession out on strike. That is not the right form for it. The book does it better; we will fall back on the book and have a cake-walk:

"It was easy to divine that some restless grief possessed him; Mary herself was not unlearned in the lore of pain. His generous zeal in her father's behalf, his spiritual sonship to
Godwin, his reverence for her mother's memory, were guarantees with Mary of his excellence.--[What she was after was guarantees of his excellence. That he stood ready to desert his wife and child was one of them, apparently.]-- The new friends could not lack subjects of discourse, and underneath heir words about Mary's mother, and 'Political Justice,' and 'Rights of Woman,' were two young hearts, each feeling towards the other, each perhaps unaware, trembling in the direction of the other. The desire to assuage the suffering of one whose happiness has grown precious to us may become a hunger of the spirit as keen as any other, and this hunger now possessed
Mary's heart; when her eyes rested unseen on Shelley, it was with a look full of the ardor of a 'soothing pity.'"

Yes, that is better and has more composure. That is just the way it happened. He told her about the wet-nurse, she told him about political justice; he told her about the deadly sister-in-law, she told him about her mother; he told her about the bonnet-shop, she murmured back about the rights of woman; then he assuaged her, then she assuaged him; then he assuaged her some more, next she assuaged him some more; then they both assuaged one another simultaneously; and so they went on by the hour assuaging and assuaging and assuaging, until at last what was the result? They were in love. It will happen so every time.

"He had married a woman who, as he now persuaded himself, had never truly loved him, who loved only his fortune and his rank, and who proved her selfishness by deserting him in his misery."
I think that that is not quite fair to Harriet. We have no certainty that she knew Cornelia had turned him out of the house. He went back to Cornelia, and Harriet may have supposed that he was as happy with her as ever. Still,

it was judicious to begin to lay on the whitewash, for Shelley is going to need many a coat of it now, and the sooner the reader becomes used to the intrusion of the brush the sooner he will get reconciled to it and stop fretting about it.

After Shelley's (conjectured) visit to Harriet at Bath--8th of June to 18th-- "it seems to have been arranged that Shelley should henceforth join the Skinner Street household each day at dinner."

Nothing could be handier than this; things will swim along now.

> *"Although now Shelley was coming to believe that his wedded union with Harriet was a thing of the past, he had not ceased to regard her with affectionate consideration; he wrote to her frequently, and kept her informed of his whereabouts."*

We must not get impatient over these curious inharmoniousnesses and irreconcilabilities in Shelley's character. You can see by the biographer's attitude towards them that there is nothing objectionable about them. Shelley was doing his best to make two adoring young creatures happy: he was regarding the one with affectionate consideration by mail, and he was assuaging the other one at home.

> *"Unhappy Harriet, residing at Bath, had perhaps never desired that the breach between herself and her husband should be irreparable and complete."*

I find no fault with that sentence except that the "perhaps" is not strictly warranted. It should have been left out. In support--or shall we say extenuation? --of this opinion I submit that there is not sufficient evidence to warrant the uncertainty which it implies. The only "evidence" offered that Harriet was hard and proud and standing out against a reconciliation is a poem--the poem in which Shelley beseeches her to "bid the remorseless feeling flee" and "pity" if she "cannot love." We have just that as "evidence," and out of its meagre materials the biographer builds a cobhouse of conjectures as big as the Coliseum; conjectures which convince him, the prosecuting attorney, but ought to fall far short of convincing any fair-minded jury.

Shelley's love-poems may be very good evidence, but we know well that they are "good for this day and train only." We are able to believe that they spoke the truth for that one day, but we know by experience that they could not be depended on to speak it the next. The very supplication for a rewarming of Harriet's chilled love was followed so suddenly by the poet's plunge into an adoring passion for Mary Godwin that if it had been a check it would have lost its value before a lazy person could have gotten to the bank with it.

Hardness, stubbornness, pride, vindictiveness--these may sometimes reside in a young wife and mother of nineteen, but they are not charged against Harriet Shelley outside of that poem, and one has no right to insert them into her character on such shadowy "evidence" as that. Peacock knew Harriet well, and she has a flexible and persuadable look, as painted by him:

"Her manners were good, and her whole aspect and demeanor such manifest emanations of pure and truthful nature that to be once in her company was to know her thoroughly. She was fond of her husband, and accommodated herself in every way to his tastes.
If they mixed in society, she adorned it; if they lived in retirement, she was satisfied; if they travelled, she enjoyed the change of scene."

"Perhaps" she had never desired that the breach should be irreparable and complete. The truth is, we do not even know that there was any breach at all at this time. We know that the husband and wife went before the altar and took a new oath on the 24th of March to love and cherish each other until death--and this may be regarded as a sort of reconciliation itself, and a wiping out of the old grudges. Then Harriet went away, and the sister-in-law removed herself from her society. That was in April. Shelley wrote his "appeal" in May, but the corresponding went right along afterwards. We have a right to doubt that the subject of it was a "reconciliation," or that Harriet had any suspicion that she needed to be reconciled and that her husband was trying to persuade her to it--as the biographer has sought to make us believe, with his Coliseum of conjectures built out of a waste-basket of poetry. For we have "evidence" now--not poetry and conjecture. When Shelley had been dining daily in the Skinner Street paradise fifteen days and continuing the love-match which was already a fortnight old twenty-five days earlier, he forgot to write Harriet; forgot it the next day and the next. During four days Harriet got no letter from him. Then her fright and anxiety rose to expression-heat, and she wrote a letter to Shelley's publisher which seems to reveal to us that Shelley's letters to her had been the customary affectionate letters of husband to wife, and had carried no appeals for reconciliation and had not needed to:

Mark Twain

"BATH (postmark July 7, 1814).
"MY DEAR SIR,-- You will greatly oblige me by giving the enclosed to Mr. Shelley.
I would not trouble you, but it is now four days since I have heard from him, which
to me is an age. Will you write by return of post and tell me what has become of
him? as I always fancy something dreadful has happened if I do not hear from him.
If you tell me that he is well I shall not come to London, but if I do not hear from
you or him I shall certainly come, as I cannot endure this dreadful state of suspense.
You are his friend and you can feel for me.
"I remain yours truly,
"H. S."

Even without Peacock's testimony that "her whole aspect and demeanor were manifest emanations of a pure and truthful nature," we should hold this to be a truthful letter, a sincere letter, a loving letter; it bears those marks; I think it is also the letter of a person accustomed to receiving letters from her husband frequently, and that they have been of a welcome and satisfactory sort, too, this long time back--ever since the solemn remarriage and reconciliation at the altar most likely.

The biographer follows Harriet's letter with a conjecture. He conjectures that she "would now gladly have retraced her steps." Which means that it is proven that she had steps to retrace--proven by the poem. Well, if the poem is better evidence than the letter, we must let it stand at that.

Then the biographer attacks Harriet Shelley's honor--by authority of random and unverified gossip scavengered from a group of people whose very names make a person shudder: Mary Godwin, mistress to Shelley; her part-sister, discarded mistress of Lord Byron; Godwin, the philosophical tramp, who gathers his share of it from a shadow--that is to say, from a person whom he shirks out of naming. Yet the biographer dignifies this sorry rubbish with the name of "evidence."

Nothing remotely resembling a distinct charge from a named person professing to know is offered among this precious "evidence."

1. "Shelley believed" so and so.

2. Byron's discarded mistress says that Shelley told Mary Godwin so and so, and Mary told her.

3. "Shelley said" so and so--and later "admitted over and over again that he had been in error."

4. The unspeakable Godwin "wrote to Mr. Baxter" that he knew so and so "from unquestionable authority"--name not furnished.

How-any man in his right mind could bring himself to defile the grave of a shamefully abused and defenceless girl with these baseless fabrications, this manufactured filth, is inconceivable. How any man, in his right mind or out of it, could sit down and coldly try to persuade anybody to believe it, or listen patiently to it, or, indeed, do anything but scoff at it and deride it, is astonishing.

The charge insinuated by these odious slanders is one of the most difficult of all offences to prove; it is also one which no man has a right to mention even in a whisper about any woman, living or dead, unless he knows it to be true, and not even then unless he can also prove it to be true. There is no justification for the abomination of putting this stuff in the book.

Against Harriet Shelley's good name there is not one scrap of tarnishing evidence, and not even a scrap of evil gossip, that comes from a source that entitles it to a hearing.

On the credit side of the account we have strong opinions from the people who knew her best. Peacock says:

"I feel it due to the memory of Harriet to state my most decided conviction that her conduct as a wife was as pure, as true, as absolutely faultless, as that of any who for such conduct are held most in honor."
Thornton Hunt, who had picked and published slight flaws in Harriet's character, says, as regards this alleged large one:
"There is not a trace of evidence or a whisper of scandal against her before her voluntary departure from Shelley."
Trelawney says:
"I was assured by the evidence of the few friends who knew both Shelley and his wife--Hookham, Hogg, Peacock, and one of the Godwins--that Harriet was perfectly innocent of all offence."

What excuse was there for raking up a parcel of foul rumors from malicious and discredited sources and flinging them at this dead girl's head? Her very defencelessness should have been her protection. The fact that all letters to her or about her, with almost every scrap of her own writing, had been diligently mislaid, leaving her case destitute of a voice, while every pen-stroke which could help her husband's side had been as diligently preserved, should have excused her from being brought to trial. Her witnesses have all disappeared, yet we see her summoned in her grave-clothes to plead for the life of her character, without the help of an advocate, before a disqualified judge and a packed jury.

Harriet Shelley wrote her distressed letter on the 7th of July. On the 28th her husband ran away with Mary Godwin and her part-sister Claire to the Continent. He deserted his wife when her confinement was approaching. She bore him a child at the end of November, his mistress bore him another one something over two months later. The truants were back in London before either of these events occurred.

On one occasion, presently, Shelley was so pressed for money to support his mistress with that he went to his wife and got some money of his that was in her hands--twenty pounds. Yet the mistress was not moved to gratitude; for later, when the wife was troubled to meet her engagements, the mistress makes this entry in her diary:

"Harriet sends her creditors here; nasty woman. Now we shallhave to change our lodgings."

The deserted wife bore the bitterness and obloquy of her situation two years and a quarter; then she gave up, and drowned herself. A month afterwards the body was found in the water. Three weeks later Shelley married his mistress.

I must here be allowed to italicize a remark of the biographer's concerning Harriet Shelley:

"That no act of Shelley's during the two years which immediately preceded her death tended to cause the rash act which brought her life to its close seems certain."

Yet her husband had deserted her and her children, and was living with a concubine all that time! Why should a person attempt to write biography when the simplest facts have no meaning to him? This book is littered with as crass stupidities as that one--deductions by the page which bear no discoverable kinship to their premises.

The biographer throws off that extraordinary remark without any perceptible disturbance to his serenity; for he follows it with a sentimental justification of Shelley's conduct which has not a pang of conscience in it, but is silky and smooth and undulating and pious-- a cake-walk with all the colored brethren at their best. There may be people who can read that page and keep their temper, but it is doubtful. Shelley's life has the one indelible blot upon it, but is otherwise worshipfully noble and beautiful. It even stands out indestructibly gracious and lovely from the ruck of these disastrous pages, in spite of the fact that they expose and establish his responsibility for his forsaken wife's pitiful fate--a responsibility which he himself tacitly admits in a letter to Eliza Westbrook, wherein he refers to his taking up with Mary Godwin as an act which Eliza "might excusably regard as the cause of her sister's ruin."

HOW TO TELL A STORY

By: Mark Twain

How To Tell A Story

Mark Twain

INTRODUCTION

The Humorous Story an American Development.--Its Difference from Comic and Witty Stories.

I do not claim that I can tell a story as it ought to be told. I only claim to know how a story ought to be told, for I have been almost daily in the company of the most expert story-tellers for many years.

There are several kinds of stories, but only one difficult kind--the humorous. I will talk mainly about that one. The humorous story is American, the comic story is English, the witty story is French. The humorous story depends for its effect upon the manner of the telling; the comic story and the witty story upon the matter.

The humorous story may be spun out to great length, and may wander around as much as it pleases, and arrive nowhere in particular; but the comic and witty stories must be brief and end with a point. The humorous story bubbles gently along, the others burst.

The humorous story is strictly a work of art--high and delicate art --and only an artist can tell it; but no art is necessary in telling the comic and the witty story; anybody can do it. The art of telling a humorous story--understand, I mean by word of mouth, not print--was created in America, and has remained at home.

The humorous story is told gravely; the teller does his best to conceal the fact that he even dimly suspects that there is anything funny about it; but the teller of the comic story tells you beforehand that it is one of the funniest things he has ever heard, then tells it with eager delight, and is the first person to laugh when he gets through. And sometimes, if he has had good success, he is so glad and happy that he will repeat the "nub" of it and glance around from face to face, collecting applause, and then repeat it again. It is a pathetic thing to see.

Very often, of course, the rambling and disjointed humorous story finishes with a nub, point, snapper, or whatever you like to call it. Then the listener must be alert, for in many cases the teller will divert attention from that nub by dropping it in a carefully casual and indifferent way, with the pretence that he does not know it is a nub.

Artemus Ward used that trick a good deal; then when the belated audience presently caught the joke he would look up with innocent surprise, as if wondering what they had found to laugh at. Dan Setchell used it before him, Nye and Riley and others use it to-day.

But the teller of the comic story does not slur the nub; he shouts it at you-- every time. And when he prints it, in England, France, Germany, and Italy, he italicizes it, puts some whooping exclamation-points after it, and sometimes explains it in a parenthesis. All of which is very depressing, and makes one want to renounce joking and lead a better life.

Let me set down an instance of the comic method, using an anecdote which has been popular all over the world for twelve or fifteen hundred years. The teller tells it in this way:

Mark Twain

THE WOUNDED SOLDIER.

In the course of a certain battle a soldier whose leg had been shot off appealed to another soldier who was hurrying by to carry him to the rear, informing him at the same time of the loss which he had sustained; whereupon the generous son of Mars, shouldering the unfortunate, proceeded to carry out his desire. The bullets and cannon-balls were flying in all directions, and presently one of the latter took the wounded man's head off--without, however, his deliverer being aware of it. In no-long time he was hailed by an officer, who said:

"Where are you going with that carcass?"

"To the rear, sir--he's lost his leg!"

"His leg, forsooth?" responded the astonished officer; "you mean his head, you booby."

Whereupon the soldier dispossessed himself of his burden, and stood looking down upon it in great perplexity. At length he said:

"It is true, sir, just as you have said." Then after a pause he added, "But he TOLD me IT WAS HIS LEG! ! ! ! !"

Here the narrator bursts into explosion after explosion of thunderous horse-laughter, repeating that nub from time to time through his gaspings and shriekings and suffocatings.

It takes only a minute and a half to tell that in its comic-story form; and isn't worth the telling, after all. Put into the humorous-story form it takes ten minutes, and is about the funniest thing I have ever listened to--as James Whitcomb Riley tells it.

He tells it in the character of a dull-witted old farmer who has just heard it for the first time, thinks it is unspeakably funny, and is trying to repeat it to a neighbor. But he can't remember it; so he gets all mixed up and wanders helplessly round and round, putting in tedious details that don't belong in the tale and only retard it; taking them out conscientiously and putting in others that are just as useless; making minor mistakes now and then and stopping to correct them and explain how he came to make them; remembering things which he forgot to put in in their proper place and going back to put them in there; stopping his narrative a good while in order to try to recall the name of the soldier that was hurt, and finally remembering that the soldier's name was not mentioned, and remarking placidly that the name is of no real importance, anyway--better, of course, if one knew it, but not essential, after all --and so on, and so on, and so on.

The teller is innocent and happy and pleased with himself, and has to stop every little while to hold himself in and keep from laughing outright; and does hold in, but his body quakes in a jelly-like way with interior chuckles; and at the end of the ten minutes the audience have laughed until they are exhausted, and the tears are running down their faces.

The simplicity and innocence and sincerity and unconsciousness of the old farmer are perfectly simulated, and the result is a performance which is thoroughly charming and delicious. This is art and fine and beautiful, and only a master can compass it; but a machine could tell the other story.

To string incongruities and absurdities together in a wandering and sometimes purposeless way, and seem innocently unaware that they are absurdities, is the basis of the American art, if my position is correct. Another feature is the slurring of the point. A third is the dropping of a studied remark apparently without knowing it, as if one were thinking aloud. The fourth and last is the pause.

Artemus Ward dealt in numbers three and four a good deal. He would begin to tell with great animation something which he seemed to think was wonderful; then lose confidence, and after an apparently absent-minded pause add an incongruous remark in a soliloquizing way; and that was the remark intended to explode the mine--and it did.

For instance, he would say eagerly, excitedly, "I once knew a man in New Zealand who hadn't a tooth in his head"--here his animation would die out; a silent, reflective pause would follow, then he would say dreamily, and as if to himself, "and yet that man could beat a drum better than any man I ever saw."

The pause is an exceedingly important feature in any kind of story, and a frequently recurring feature, too. It is a dainty thing, and delicate, and also uncertain and treacherous; for it must be exactly the right length--no more and no less--or it fails of its purpose and makes trouble. If the pause is too short the impressive point is passed, and [and if too long] the audience have had time to divine that a surprise is intended--and then you can't surprise them, of course.

On the platform I used to tell a negro ghost story that had a pause in front of the snapper on the end, and that pause was the most important thing in the whole story. If I got it the right length precisely, I could spring the finishing ejaculation with effect enough to make some impressible girl deliver a startled little yelp and jump out of her seat --and that was what I was after. This story was called "The Golden Arm," and was told in this fashion. You can practise with it yourself--and mind you look out for the pause and get it right.

How To Tell A Story

Mark Twain

THE GOLDEN ARM.

Once 'pon a time dey wuz a monsus mean man, en he live 'way out in de prairie all 'lone by hisself, 'cep'n he had a wife. En bimeby she died, en he tuck en toted her way out dah in de prairie en buried her. Well, she had a golden arm--all solid gold, fum de shoulder down. He wuz pow'ful mean--pow'ful; en dat night he couldn't sleep, Gaze he want dat golden arm so bad.

When it come midnight he couldn't stan' it no mo'; so he git up, he did, en tuck his lantern en shoved out thoo de storm en dug her up en got de golden arm; en he bent his head down 'gin de win', en plowed en plowed en plowed thoo de snow. Den all on a sudden he stop (make a considerable pause here, and look startled, and take a listening attitude) en say: "My LAN', what's dat!"

En he listen--en listen--en de win' say (set your teeth together and imitate the wailing and wheezing singsong of the wind), "Bzzz-z-zzz" --en den, way back yonder whah de grave is, he hear a voice! he hear a voice all mix' up in de win' can't hardly tell 'em 'part--"Bzzz-zzz --W-h-o--g-o-t--m-y--g-o-l-d-e-n arm?--zzz--zzz--W-h-o g-o-t m-y g-o-l-d-e-n arm!" (You must begin to shiver violently now.)

En he begin to shiver en shake, en say, "Oh, my! OH, my lan'!" en de win' blow de lantern out, en de snow en sleet blow in his face en mos' choke him, en he start a-plowin' knee-deep towards home mos' dead, he so sk'yerd--en pooty soon he hear de voice agin, en (pause) it 'us comin' after him! "Bzzz--zzz--zzz--W-h-o--g-o-t m-y--g-o-l-d-e-n--arm?"

When he git to de pasture he hear it agin closter now, en a-comin'! --a-comin' back dah in de dark en de storm--(repeat the wind and the voice). When he git to de house he rush up-stairs en jump in de bed en kiver up, head and years, en lay dah shiverin' en shakin'--en den way out dah he hear it agin!--en a-comin'! En bimeby he hear (pause--awed, listening attitude)-- pat--pat--pat--hit's acomin' up-stairs! Den he hear de latch, en he know it's in de room!

Den pooty soon he know it's a-stannin' by de bed! (Pause.) Den--he know it's a-bendin' down over him--en he cain't skasely git his breath! Den --den-- he seem to feel someth' n c-o-l-d, right down 'most agin his head! (Pause.)

Den de voice say, right at his year--"W-h-o g-o-t--m-y--g-o-l-d-e-n arm?" (You must wail it out very plaintively and accusingly; then you stare steadily and impressively into the face of the farthest-gone auditor--a girl, preferably--and let that awe-inspiring pause begin to build itself in the deep hush. When it has reached exactly the right length, jump suddenly at that girl and yell, "You've got it!")

If you've got the pause right, she'll fetch a dear little yelp and spring right out of her shoes. But you must get the pause right; and you will find it the most troublesome and aggravating and uncertain thing you ever undertook.

Mark Twain

MENTAL TELEGRAPHY AGAIN.

I have three or four curious incidents to tell about. They seem to come under the head of what I named "Mental Telegraphy" in a paper written seventeen years ago, and published long afterwards.--[The paper entitled "Mental Telegraphy," which originally appeared in Harper's Magazine for December, 1893, is included in the volume entitled The American Claimant and Other Stories and Sketches.]

Several years ago I made a campaign on the platform with Mr. George W. Cable. In Montreal we were honored with a reception. It began at two in the afternoon in a long drawing-room in the Windsor Hotel. Mr. Cable and I stood at one end of this room, and the ladies and gentlemen entered it at the other end, crossed it at that end, then came up the long left-hand side, shook hands with us, said a word or two, and passed on, in the usual way. My sight is of the telescopic sort, and I presently recognized a familiar face among the throng of strangers drifting in at the distant door, and I said to myself, with surprise and high gratification, "That is Mrs. R.; I had forgotten that she was a Canadian." She had been a great friend of mine in Carson City, Nevada, in the early days. I had not seen her or heard of her for twenty years; I had not been thinking about her; there was nothing to suggest her to me, nothing to bring her to my mind; in fact, to me she had long ago ceased to exist, and had disappeared from my consciousness. But I knew her instantly; and I saw her so clearly that I was able to note some of the particulars of her dress, and did note them, and they remained in my mind. I was impatient for her to come. In the midst of the hand-shakings I snatched glimpses of her and noted her progress with the slow-moving file across the end of the room; then I saw her start up the side, and this gave me a full front view of her face. I saw her last when she was within twenty-five feet of me. For an hour I kept thinking she must still be in the room somewhere and would come at last, but I was disappointed.

When I arrived in the lecture-hall that evening some one said: "Come into the waiting-room; there's a friend of yours there who wants to see you. You'll not be introduced--you are to do the recognizing without help if you can."

I said to myself: "It is Mrs. R.; I shan't have any trouble."

There were perhaps ten ladies present, all seated. In the midst of them was Mrs. R., as I had expected. She was dressed exactly as she was when I had seen her in the afternoon. I went forward and shook hands with her and called her by name, and said:

"I knew you the moment you appeared at the reception this afternoon." She looked surprised, and said: "But I was not at the reception. I have just arrived from Quebec, and have not been in town an hour."

It was my turn to be surprised now. I said: "I can't help it. I give you my word of honor that it is as I say. I saw you at the reception, and you were dressed precisely as you are now. When they told me a moment ago that I should find a friend in this room, your image rose before me, dress and all, just as I had seen you at the reception."

Those are the facts. She was not at the reception at all, or anywhere near it; but I saw her there nevertheless, and most clearly and unmistakably. To that I could make oath. How is one to explain this? I was not thinking of her at the time; had not thought of her for years. But she had been thinking of me, no doubt; did her thoughts flit through leagues of air to me, and bring with it that clear and pleasant vision of herself? I think so. That was and remains my sole experience in the matter of apparitions--I mean apparitions that come when one is (ostensibly) awake. I could have been asleep for a moment; the apparition could have been the creature of a dream. Still, that is nothing to the point; the feature of interest is the happening of the thing just at that time, instead of at an earlier or later time, which is argument that its origin lay in thought-transference.

My next incident will be set aside by most persons as being merely a "coincidence," I suppose. Years ago I used to think sometimes of making a lecturing trip through the antipodes and the borders of the Orient, but always gave up the idea, partly because of the great length of the journey and partly because my wife could not well manage to go with me. Towards the end of last January that idea, after an interval of years, came suddenly into my head again--forcefully, too, and without any apparent reason. Whence came it? What suggested it? I will touch upon that presently.

I was at that time where I am now--in Paris. I wrote at once to Henry M. Stanley (London), and asked him some questions about his Australian lecture tour, and inquired who had conducted him and what were the terms. After a day or two his answer came. It began:

"The lecture agent for Australia and New Zealand is par excellence Mr. R. S. Smythe, of Melbourne."

He added his itinerary, terms, sea expenses, and some other matters, and advised me to write Mr. Smythe, which I did--February 3d. I began my letter by saying in substance that while he did not know me personally we had a mutual friend in Stanley, and that would answer for an introduction. Then I proposed my trip, and asked if he would give me the same terms which he had given Stanley.

I mailed my letter to Mr. Smythe February 6th, and three days later I got a letter from the selfsame Smythe, dated Melbourne, December 17th. I would as soon have expected to get a letter from the late George Washington. The letter began somewhat as mine to him had begun--with a self-introduction:

"DEAR MR. CLEMENS,--It is so long since Archibald Forbes and I spent that pleasant afternoon in your comfortable house at Hartford that you have probably quite forgotten the occasion."

In the course of his letter this occurs:

"I am willing to give you" [here he named the terms which he had given Stanley] "for an antipodean tour to last, say, three months."

Here was the single essential detail of my letter answered three days after I had mailed my inquiry. I might have saved myself the trouble and the postage--and a few years ago I would have done that very thing, for I would have argued that my sudden and strong impulse to write and ask some questions of a stranger on the under side of the globe meant that the impulse came from that stranger, and that he would answer my questions of his own motion if I would let him alone.

Mr. Smythe's letter probably passed under my nose on its way to lose three weeks traveling to America and back, and gave me a whiff of its contents as it went along. Letters often act like that. Instead of the thought coming to you in an instant from Australia, the (apparently) unsentient letter imparts it to you as it glides invisibly past your elbow in the mail-bag.

Next incident. In the following month--March--I was in America. I spent a Sunday at Irvington-on-the-Hudson with Mr. John Brisben Walker, of the Cosmopolitan magazine. We came into New York next morning, and went to the Century Club for luncheon. He said some praiseful things about the character of the club and the orderly serenity and pleasantness of its quarters, and asked if I had never tried to acquire membership in it. I said I had not, and that New York clubs were a continuous expense to the country members without being of frequent use or benefit to them.

"And now I've got an idea!" said I. "There's the Lotos--the first New York club I was ever a member of--my very earliest love in that line. I have been a member of it for considerably more than twenty years, yet have seldom had a chance to look in and see the boys. They turn gray and grow old while I am not watching. And my dues go on. I am going to Hartford this afternoon for a day or two, but as soon as I get back I will go to John Elderkin very privately and say: 'Remember the veteran and confer distinction upon him, for the sake of old times. Make me an honorary member and abolish the tax. If you haven't any such thing as honorary membership, all the better--create it for my honor and glory.' That would be a great thing; I will go to John Elderkin as soon as I get back from Hartford."

I took the last express that afternoon, first telegraphing Mr. F. G. Whitmore to come and see me next day. When he came he asked: "Did you get a letter from Mr. John Elderkin, secretary of the Lotos Club, before you left New York?"

"Then it just missed you. If I had known you were coming I would have kept it. It is beautiful, and will make you proud. The Board of Directors, by unanimous vote, have made you a life member, and squelched those dues;

and, you are to be on hand and receive your distinction on the night of the 30th, which is the twenty-fifth anniversary of the founding of the club, and it will not surprise me if they have some great times there."

What put the honorary membership in my head that day in the Century Club? for I had never thought of it before. I don't know what brought the thought to me at that particular time instead of earlier, but I am well satisfied that it originated with the Board of Directors, and had been on its way to my brain through the air ever since the moment that saw their vote recorded.

Another incident. I was in Hartford two or three days as a guest of the Rev. Joseph H. Twichell. I have held the rank of Honorary Uncle to his children for a quarter of a century, and I went out with him in the trolley-car to visit one of my nieces, who is at Miss Porter's famous school in Farmington. The distance is eight or nine miles. On the way, talking, I illustrated something with an anecdote. This is the anecdote:

Two years and a half ago I and the family arrived at Milan on our way to Rome, and stopped at the Continental. After dinner I went below and took a seat in the stone-paved court, where the customary lemon-trees stand in the customary tubs, and said to myself, "Now this is comfort, comfort and repose, and nobody to disturb it; I do not know anybody in Milan."

Then a young gentleman stepped up and shook hands, which damaged my theory. He said, in substance:

"You won't remember me, Mr. Clemens, but I remember you very well. I was a cadet at West Point when you and Rev. Joseph H. Twichell came there some years ago and talked to us on a Hundredth Night. I am a lieutenant in the regular army now, and my name is H. I am in Europe, all alone, for a modest little tour; my regiment is in Arizona."

We became friendly and sociable, and in the course of the talk he told me of an adventure which had befallen him--about to this effect:

"I was at Bellagio, stopping at the big hotel there, and ten days ago I lost my letter of credit. I did not know what in the world to do. I was a stranger; I knew no one in Europe; I hadn't a penny in my pocket; I couldn't even send a telegram to London to get my lost letter replaced; my hotel bill was a week old, and the presentation of it imminent--so imminent that it could happen at any moment now. I was so frightened that my wits seemed to leave me. I tramped and tramped, back and forth, like a crazy person. If anybody approached me I hurried away, for no matter what a person looked like, I took him for the head waiter with the bill.

"I was at last in such a desperate state that I was ready to do any wild thing that promised even the shadow of help, and so this is the insane thing that I did. I saw a family lunching at a small table on the veranda, and recognized their nationality--Americans--father, mother, and several young daughters-- young, tastefully dressed, and pretty--the rule with our people. I went straight there in my civilian costume, named my name, said I was a lieutenant in the army, and told my story and asked for help.

"What do you suppose the gentleman did? But you would not guess in twenty years. He took out a handful of gold coin and told me to help myself--freely. That is what he did."

The next morning the lieutenant told me his new letter of credit had arrived in the night, so we strolled to Cook's to draw money to pay back the benefactor with. We got it, and then went strolling through the great arcade. Presently he said, "Yonder they are; come and be introduced." I was introduced to the parents and the young ladies; then we separated, and I never saw him or them any m---

"Here we are at Farmington," said Twichell, interrupting.

We left the trolley-car and tramped through the mud a hundred yards or so to the school, talking about the time we and Warner walked out there years ago, and the pleasant time we had.

We had a visit with my niece in the parlor, then started for the trolley again. Outside the house we encountered a double rank of twenty or thirty of Miss Porter's young ladies arriving from a walk, and we stood aside, ostensibly to let them have room to file past, but really to look at them. Presently one of them stepped out of the rank and said:

"You don't know me, Mr. Twichell; but I know your daughter, and that gives me the privilege of shaking hands with you."

Then she put out her hand to me, and said:

"And I wish to shake hands with you too, Mr. Clemens. You don't remember me, but you were introduced to me in the arcade in Milan two years and a half ago by Lieutenant H."

What had put that story into my head after all that stretch of time? Was it just the proximity of that young girl, or was it merely an odd accident?

How To Tell A Story

Mark Twain

THE INVALID'S STORY.

I seem sixty and married, but these effects are due to my condition and sufferings, for I am a bachelor, and only forty-one. It will be hard for you to believe that I, who am now but a shadow, was a hale, hearty man two short years ago, a man of iron, a very athlete!--yet such is the simple truth. But stranger still than this fact is the way in which I lost my health. I lost it through helping to take care of a box of guns on a two-hundred-mile railway journey one winter's night. It is the actual truth, and I will tell you about it.

I belong in Cleveland, Ohio. One winter's night, two years ago, I reached home just after dark, in a driving snow-storm, and the first thing I heard when I entered the house was that my dearest boyhood friend and schoolmate, John B. Hackett, had died the day before, and that his last utterance had been a desire that I would take his remains home to his poor old father and mother in Wisconsin. I was greatly shocked and grieved, but there was no time to waste in emotions; I must start at once. I took the card, marked "Deacon Levi Hackett, Bethlehem, Wisconsin," and hurried off through the whistling storm to the railway station. Arrived there I found the long white-pine box which had been described to me; I fastened the card to it with some tacks, saw it put safely aboard the express car, and then ran into the eating-room to provide myself with a sandwich and some cigars. When I returned, presently, there was my coffin-box back again, apparently, and a young fellow examining around it, with a card in his hands, and some tacks and a hammer! I was astonished and puzzled. He began to nail on his card, and I rushed out to the express car, in a good deal of a state of mind, to ask for an explanation. But no--there was my box, all right, in the express car; it hadn't been disturbed. [The fact is that without my suspecting it a prodigious mistake had been made. I was carrying off a box of guns which that young fellow had come to the station to ship to a rifle company in

Peoria, Illinois, and he had got my corpse!] Just then the conductor sung out "All aboard," and I jumped into the express car and got a comfortable seat on a bale of buckets. The expressman was there, hard at work,--a plain man of fifty, with a simple, honest, good-natured face, and a breezy, practical heartiness in his general style. As the train moved off a stranger skipped into the car and set a package of peculiarly mature and capable Limburger cheese on one end of my coffin-box--I mean my box of guns. That is to say, I know now that it was Limburger cheese, but at that time I never had heard of the article in my life, and of course was wholly ignorant of its character. Well, we sped through the wild night, the bitter storm raged on, a cheerless misery stole over me, my heart went down, down, down! The old expressman made a brisk remark or two about the tempest and the arctic weather, slammed his sliding doors to, and bolted them, closed his window down tight, and then went bustling around, here and there and yonder, setting things to rights, and all the time contentedly humming "Sweet By and By," in a low tone, and flatting a good deal. Presently I began to detect a most evil and searching odor stealing about on the frozen air. This depressed my spirits still more, because of course I attributed it to my poor departed friend. There was something infinitely saddening about his calling himself to my remembrance in this dumb pathetic way, so it was hard to keep the tears back. Moreover, it distressed me on account of the old expressman, who, I was afraid, might notice it. However, he went humming tranquilly on, and gave no sign; and for this I was grateful. Grateful, yes, but still uneasy; and soon I began to feel more and more uneasy every minute, for every minute that went by that odor thickened up the more, and got to be more and more gamey and hard to stand. Presently, having got things arranged to his satisfaction, the expressman got some wood and made up a tremendous fire in his stove.

This distressed me more than I can tell, for I could not but feel that it was a mistake. I was sure that the effect would be deleterious upon my poor departed friend. Thompson--the expressman's name was Thompson, as I found out in the course of the night--now went poking around his car, stopping up whatever stray cracks he could find, remarking that it didn't make any difference what kind of a night it was outside, he calculated to make us comfortable, anyway. I said nothing, but I believed he was not choosing the right way. Meantime he was humming to himself just as before; and meantime, too, the stove was getting hotter and hotter, and the place closer and closer. I felt myself growing pale and qualmish, but grieved in silence and said nothing.

Soon I noticed that the "Sweet By and By" was gradually fading out; next it ceased altogether, and there was an ominous stillness. After a few moments Thompson said,

"Pfew! I reckon it ain't no cinnamon 't I've loaded up thish-yer stove with!"

He gasped once or twice, then moved toward the cof--gun-box, stood over that Limburger cheese part of a moment, then came back and sat down near me, looking a good deal impressed. After a contemplative pause, he said, indicating the box with a gesture,

"Friend of yourn?"

"Yes," I said with a sigh.

"He's pretty ripe, ain't he!"

Nothing further was said for perhaps a couple of minutes, each being busy with his own thoughts; then Thompson said, in a low, awed voice,

"Sometimes it's uncertain whether they're really gone or not,--seem gone, you know--body warm, joints limber--and so, although you think they're gone, you don't really know. I've had cases in my car. It's perfectly awful, becuz you don't know what minute they'll rise up and look at you!" Then, after a pause, and slightly lifting his elbow toward the box, --"But he ain't in no trance! No, sir, I go bail for him!"

We sat some time, in meditative silence, listening to the wind and the roar of the train; then Thompson said, with a good deal of feeling,

"Well-a-well, we've all got to go, they ain't no getting around it. Man that is born of woman is of few days and far between, as Scriptur' says. Yes, you look at it any way you want to, it's awful solemn and cur'us: they ain't nobody can get around it; all's got to go--just everybody, as you may say. One day you're hearty and strong"--here he scrambled to his feet and broke a pane and stretched his nose out at it a moment or two, then sat down again while I struggled up and thrust my nose out at the same place, and this we kept on doing every now and then--"and next day he's cut down like the grass, and the places which knowed him then knows him no more forever, as Scriptur' says. Yes'ndeedy, it's awful solemn and cur'us; but we've all got to go, one time or another; they ain't no getting around it."

There was another long pause; then,--

"What did he die of?"

I said I didn't know.

"How long has he ben dead?"

It seemed judicious to enlarge the facts to fit the probabilities; so I said,

"Two or three days."

But it did no good; for Thompson received it with an injured look which plainly said, "Two or three years, you mean." Then he went right along, placidly ignoring my statement, and gave his views at considerable length upon the unwisdom of putting off burials too long. Then he lounged off toward the box, stood a moment, then came back on a sharp trot and visited the broken pane, observing,

"'Twould 'a' ben a dum sight better, all around, if they'd started him along last summer."

Thompson sat down and buried his face in his red silk handkerchief, and began to slowly sway and rock his body like one who is doing his best to endure the almost unendurable. By this time the fragrance--if you may call it fragrance--was just about suffocating, as near as you can come at it. Thompson's face was turning gray; I knew mine hadn't any color left in it. By and by Thompson rested his forehead in his left hand, with his elbow on his knee, and sort of waved his red handkerchief towards the box with his other hand, and said,--

"I've carried a many a one of 'em,--some of 'em considerable overdue, too,-- but, lordy, he just lays over 'em all!--and does it easy Cap., they was heliotrope to HIM!"

This recognition of my poor friend gratified me, in spite of the sad circumstances, because it had so much the sound of a compliment.

Pretty soon it was plain that something had got to be done. I suggested cigars. Thompson thought it was a good idea. He said,

"Likely it'll modify him some."

We puffed gingerly along for a while, and tried hard to imagine that things were improved. But it wasn't any use. Before very long, and without any consultation, both cigars were quietly dropped from our nerveless fingers at the same moment. Thompson said, with a sigh,

"No, Cap., it don't modify him worth a cent. Fact is, it makes him worse, becuz it appears to stir up his ambition. What do you reckon we better do, now?"

I was not able to suggest anything; indeed, I had to be swallowing and swallowing, all the time, and did not like to trust myself to speak. Thompson fell to maundering, in a desultory and low-spirited way, about the miserable experiences of this night; and he got to referring to my poor friend by various titles,--sometimes military ones, sometimes civil ones; and I noticed that as fast as my poor friend's effectiveness grew, Thompson promoted him accordingly,--gave him a bigger title. Finally he said,

"I've got an idea. Suppos' n we buckle down to it and give the Colonel a bit of a shove towards t'other end of the car?--about ten foot, say. He wouldn't have so much influence, then, don't you reckon?"

I said it was a good scheme. So we took in a good fresh breath at the broken pane, calculating to hold it till we got through; then we went there and bent over that deadly cheese and took a grip on the box. Thompson nodded "All ready," and then we threw ourselves forward with all our might; but Thompson slipped, and slumped down with his nose on the cheese, and his breath got loose. He gagged and gasped, and floundered up and made a break for the door, pawing the air and saying hoarsely, "Don't hender me!-- gimme the road! I'm a-dying; gimme the road!" Out on the cold platform I sat down and held his head a while, and he revived. Presently he said,

"Do you reckon we started the Gen'rul any?"

I said no; we hadn't budged him.

"Well, then, that idea's up the flume. We got to think up something else. He's suited wher' he is, I reckon; and if that's the way he feels about it, and has made up his mind that he don't wish to be disturbed, you bet he's a-going to have his own way in the business. Yes, better leave him right wher' he is, long as he wants it so; becuz he holds all the trumps, don't you know, and so it stands to reason that the man that lays out to alter his plans for him is going to get left."

But we couldn't stay out there in that mad storm; we should have frozen to death. So we went in again and shut the door, and began to suffer once more and take turns at the break in the window. By and by, as we were starting away from a station where we had stopped a moment Thompson. pranced in cheerily, and exclaimed,

"We're all right, now! I reckon we've got the Commodore this time. I judge I've got the stuff here that'll take the tuck out of him."

It was carbolic acid. He had a carboy of it. He sprinkled it all around everywhere; in fact he drenched everything with it, rifle-box, cheese and all. Then we sat down, feeling pretty hopeful. But it wasn't for long. You see the two perfumes began to mix, and then--well, pretty soon we made a break for the door; and out there Thompson swabbed his face with his bandanna and said in a kind of disheartened way,

"It ain't no use. We can't buck agin him. He just utilizes everything we put up to modify him with, and gives it his own flavor and plays it back on us. Why, Cap., don't you know, it's as much as a hundred times worse in there now than it was when he first got a-going. I never did see one of 'em warm up to his work so, and take such a dumnation interest in it. No, Sir, I never did, as long as I've ben on the road; and I've carried a many a one of 'em, as I was telling you."

We went in again after we were frozen pretty stiff; but my, we couldn't stay in, now. So we just waltzed back and forth, freezing, and thawing, and stifling, by turns. In about an hour we stopped at another station; and as we left it Thompson came in with a bag, and said,--

"Cap., I'm a-going to chance him once more,--just this once; and if we don't fetch him this time, the thing for us to do, is to just throw up the sponge and withdraw from the canvass. That's the way I put it up." He had brought a lot of chicken feathers, and dried apples, and leaf tobacco, and rags, and old shoes, and sulphur, and asafoetida, and one thing or another; and he, piled them on a breadth of sheet iron in the middle of the floor, and set fire to them.

When they got well started, I couldn't see, myself, how even the corpse could stand it. All that went before was just simply poetry to that smell,-- but mind you, the original smell stood up out of it just as sublime as ever,-- fact is, these other smells just seemed to give it a better hold; and my, how rich it was! I didn't make these reflections there--there wasn't time--made them on the platform. And breaking for the platform, Thompson got suffocated and fell; and before I got him dragged out, which I did by the collar, I was mighty near gone myself. When we revived, Thompson said dejectedly,--

"We got to stay out here, Cap. We got to do it. They ain't no other way. The Governor wants to travel alone, and he's fixed so he can outvote us."

And presently he added,

"And don't you know, we're pisoned. It's our last trip, you can make up your mind to it. Typhoid fever is what's going to come of this. I feel it acoming right now. Yes, sir, we're elected, just as sure as you're born."

We were taken from the platform an hour later, frozen and insensible, at the next station, and I went straight off into a virulent fever, and never knew anything again for three weeks. I found out, then, that I had spent that awful night with a harmless box of rifles and a lot of innocent cheese; but the news was too late to save me; imagination had done its work, and my health was permanently shattered; neither Bermuda nor any other land can ever bring it back tome. This is my last trip; I am on my way home to die.

How To Tell A Story

GOLDSMITH'S FRIEND ABROAD AGAIN

By: Mark Twain

NOTE.

No experience is set down in the following letters which had to be invented. Fancy is not needed to give variety to the history of a Chinaman's sojourn in America. Plain fact is amply sufficient.

Goldsmith's Friend Abroad Again

Mark Twain

LETTER I

SHANGHAI, 18--. DEAR CHING-FOO: It is all settled, and I am to leave my oppressed and overburdened native land and cross the sea to that noble realm where all are free and all equal, and none reviled or abused--America! America, whose precious privilege it is to call herself the Land of the Free and the Home of the Brave. We and all that are about us here look over the waves longingly, contrasting the privations of this our birthplace with the opulent comfort of that happy refuge. We know how America has welcomed the Germans and the Frenchmen and the stricken and sorrowing Irish, and we know how she has given them bread and work, and liberty, and how grateful they are. And we know that America stands ready to welcome all other oppressed peoples and offer her abundance to all that come, without asking what their nationality is, or their creed or color. And, without being told it, we know that the foreign sufferers she has rescued from oppression and starvation are the most eager of her children to welcome us, because, having suffered themselves, they know what suffering is, and having been generously succored, they long to be generous to other unfortunates and thus show that magnanimity is not wasted upon them.

AH SONG HI.

LETTER II

AT SEA, 18--. DEAR CHING-FOO: We are far away at sea now; on our way to the beautiful Land of the Free and Home of the Brave. We shall soon be where all men are alike, and where sorrow is not known.

The good American who hired me to go to his country is to pay me $12 a month, which is immense wages, you know--twenty times as much as one gets in China. My passage in the ship is a very large sum--indeed, it is a fortune--and this I must pay myself eventually, but I am allowed ample time to make it good to my employer in, he advancing it now. For a mere form, I have turned over my wife, my boy, and my two daughters to my employer's partner for security for the payment of the ship fare. But my employer says they are in no danger of being sold, for he knows I will be faithful to him, and that is the main security.

I thought I would have twelve dollars to, begin life with in America, but the American Consul took two of them for making a certificate that I was shipped on the steamer. He has no right to do more than charge the ship two dollars for one certificate for the ship, with the number of her Chinese passengers set down in it; but he chooses to force a certificate upon each and every Chinaman and put the two dollars in his pocket. As 1,300 of my countrymen are in this vessel, the Consul received $2,600 for certificates. My employer tells me that the Government at Washington know of this fraud, and are so bitterly opposed to the existence of such a wrong that they tried hard to have the extor--the fee, I mean, legalised by the last Congress;-- [Pacific and Mediterranean steamship bills.(Ed. Mem.)]--but as the bill did not pass, the Consul will have to take the fee dishonestly until next Congress makes it legitimate. It is a great and good and noble country, and hates all forms of vice and chicanery.

We are in that part of the vessel always reserved for my countrymen. It is called the steerage. It is kept for us, my employer says, because it is not subject to changes of temperature and dangerous drafts of air. It is only another instance of the loving unselfishness of the Americans for all unfortunate foreigners. The steerage is a little crowded, and rather warm and close, but no doubt it is best for us that it should be so.

Yesterday our people got to quarrelling among themselves, and the captain turned a volume of hot steam upon a mass of them and scalded eighty or ninety of them more or less severely. Flakes and ribbons of skin came off some of them. There was wild shrieking and struggling while the vapour enveloped the great throng, and so some who were not scalded got trampled upon and hurt. We do not complain, for my employer says this is the usual way of quieting disturbances on board the ship, and that it is done in the cabins among the Americans every day or two.

Congratulate me, Ching-Fool In ten days more I shall step upon the shore of America, and be received by her great-hearted people; and I shall straighten myself up and feel that I am a free man among freemen.

AH SONG HI.

LETTER III

SAN FRANCISCO, 18--. DEAR CHING-FOO: I stepped ashore jubilant! I wanted to dance, shout, sing, worship the generous Land of the Free and Home of the Brave. But as I walked from the gangplank a man in a gray uniform--[Policeman] --kicked me violently behind and told me to look out--so my employer translated it. As I turned, another officer of the same kind struck me with a short club and also instructed me to look out. I was about to take hold of my end of the pole which had mine and Hong-Wo's basket and things suspended from it, when a third officer hit me with his club to signify that I was to drop it, and then kicked me to signify that he was satisfied with my promptness. Another person came now, and searched all through our basket and bundles, emptying everything out on the dirty wharf. Then this person and another searched us all over. They found a little package of opium sewed into the artificial part of Hong-Wo's queue, and they took that, and also they made him prisoner and handed him over to an officer, who marched him away. They took his luggage, too, because of his crime, and as our luggage was so mixed together that they could not tell mine from his, they took it all. When I offered to help divide it, they kicked me and desired me to look out.

Having now no baggage and no companion, I told my employer that if he was willing, I would walk about a little and see the city and the people until he needed me. I did not like to seem disappointed with my reception in the good land of refuge for the oppressed, and so I looked and spoke as cheerily as I could. But he said, wait a minute--I must be vaccinated to prevent my taking the small-pox. I smiled and said I had already had the small-pox, as he could see by the marks, and so I need not wait to be "vaccinated," as he called it. But he said it was the law, and I must be vaccinated anyhow. The doctor would never let me pass, for the law obliged him to vaccinate all

Chinamen and charge them ten dollars apiece for it, and I might be sure that no doctor who would be the servant of that law would let a fee slip through his fingers to accommodate any absurd fool who had seen fit to have the disease in some other country. And presently the doctor came and did his work and took my last penny--my ten dollars which were the hard savings of nearly a year and a half of labour and privation. Ah, if the law-makers had only known there were plenty of doctors in the city glad of a chance to vaccinate people for a dollar or two, they would never have put the price up so high against a poor friendless Irish, or Italian, or Chinese pauper fleeing to the good land to escape hunger and hard times.

AH SONG HI.

LETTER IV

SAN FRANCISCO, 18--. DEAR CHING-FOO: I have been here about a month now, and am learning a little of the language every day. My employer was disappointed in the matter of hiring us out to service to the plantations in the far eastern portion of this continent. His enterprise was a failure, and so he set us all free, merely taking measures to secure to himself the repayment of the passage money which he paid for us. We are to make this good to him out of the first moneys we earn here. He says it is sixty dollars apiece.

We were thus set free about two weeks after we reached here. We had been massed together in some small houses up to that time, waiting. I walked forth to seek my fortune. I was to begin life a stranger in a strange land, without a friend, or a penny, or any clothes but those I had on my back. I had not any advantage on my side in the world--not one, except good health and the lack of any necessity to waste any time or anxiety on the watching of my baggage. No, I forget. I reflected that I had one prodigious advantage over paupers in other lands--I was in America! I was in the heaven-provided refuge of the oppressed and the forsaken!

Just as that comforting thought passed through my mind, some young men set a fierce dog on me. I tried to defend myself, but could do nothing. I retreated to the recess of a closed doorway, and there the dog had me at his mercy, flying at my throat and face or any part of my body that presented itself. I shrieked for help, but the young men only jeered and laughed. Two men in gray uniforms (policemen is their official title) looked on for a minute and then walked leisurely away. But a man stopped them and brought them back and told them it was a shame to leave me in such distress. Then the two policemen beat off the dog with small clubs, and a comfort it was to be rid of him, though I was just rags and blood from head to foot. The man who brought the policemen asked the young men why they abused me in that way, and they said they didn't want any of his meddling. And they said to him:

"This Ching divil comes till Ameriky to take the bread out o' dacent intilligent white men's mouths, and whir they try to defind their rights there's a dale o' fuss made about it."

They began to threaten my benefactor, and as he saw no friendliness in the faces that had gathered meanwhile, he went on his way. He got many a curse when he was gone. The policemen now told me I was under arrest and must go with them. I asked one of them what wrong I had done to any one that I should be arrested, and he only struck me with his club and ordered me to "hold my yap." With a jeering crowd of street boys and loafers at my heels, I was taken up an alley and into a stone-paved dungeon which had large cells all down one side of it, with iron gates to them. I stood up by a desk while a man behind it wrote down certain things about me on a slate. One of my captors said:

"Enter a charge against this Chinaman of being disorderly and disturbing the peace."

I attempted to say a word, but he said:

"Silence! Now ye had better go slow, my good fellow. This is two or three times you've tried to get off some of your d---d insolence. Lip won't do here. You've got to simmer down, and if you don't take to it paceable we'll see if we can't make you. Fat's your name?"

"Ah Song Hi."

"Alias what?"

I said I did not understand, and he said what he wanted was my true name, for he guessed I picked up this one since I stole my last chickens. They all laughed loudly at that.

Then they searched me. They found nothing, of course. They seemed very angry and asked who I supposed would "go my bail or pay my fine." When they explained these things to me, I said I had done nobody any harm, and why should I need to have bail or pay a fine? Both of them kicked me and warned me that I would find it to my advantage to try and be as civil as convenient. I protested that I had not meant anything disrespectful. Then one of them took me to one side and said:

"Now look here, Johnny, it's no use you playing softly wid us. We mane business, ye know; and the sooner ye put us on the scent of a V, the asier yell save yerself from a dale of trouble. Ye can't get out o' this for anny less. Who's your frinds?"

I told him I had not a single friend in all the land of America, and that I was far from home and help, and very poor. And I begged him to let me go.

He gathered the slack of my blouse collar in his grip and jerked and shoved and hauled at me across the dungeon, and then unlocking an iron cell-gate thrust me in with a kick and said:

"Rot there, ye furrin spawn, till ye lairn that there's no room in America for the likes of ye or your nation."

AH SONG HI.

Goldsmith's Friend Abroad Again

LETTER V

SAN FRANCISCO, 18--. DEAR CHING-FOO: You will remember that I had just been thrust violently into a cell in the city prison when I wrote last. I stumbled and fell on some one. I got a blow and a curse= and on top of these a kick or two and a shove. In a second or two it was plain that I was in a nest of prisoners and was being "passed around"--for the instant I was knocked out of the way of one I fell on the head or heels of another and was promptly ejected, only to land on a third prisoner and get a new contribution of kicks and curses and a new destination. I brought up at last in an unoccupied corner, very much battered and bruised and sore, but glad enough to be let alone for a little while. I was on the flag-stones, for there was, no furniture in the den except a long, broad board, or combination of boards, like a barn-door, and this bed was accommodating five or six persons, and that was its full capacity. They lay stretched side by side, snoring--when not fighting. One end of the board was four, inches higher than the other, and so the slant answered for a pillow. There were no blankets, and the night was a little chilly; the nights are always a little chilly in San Francisco, though never severely cold. The board was a deal more comfortable than the stones, and occasionally some flag-stone plebeian like me would try to creep to a place on it; and then the aristocrats would hammer him good and make him think a flag pavement was a nice enough place after all.

I lay quiet in my corner, stroking my bruises, and listening to the revelations the prisoners made to each other--and to me for some that were near me talked to me a good deal. I had long had an idea that Americans, being free, had no need of prisons, which are a contrivance of despots for keeping restless patriots out of mischief. So I was considerably surprised to find out my mistake.

Ours was a big general cell, it seemed, for the temporary accommodation of all comers whose crimes were trifling. Among us they were two Americans, two "Greasers" (Mexicans), a Frenchman, a German, four Irishmen, a Chilenean (and, in the next cell, only separated from us by a grating, two women), all drunk, and all more or less noisy; and as night fell and advanced, they grew more and more discontented and disorderly, occasionally; shaking the prison bars and glaring through them at the slowly pacing officer, and cursing him with all their hearts. The two women were nearly middle-aged, and they had only had enough liquor to stimulate instead of stupefy them. Consequently they would fondle and kiss each other for some minutes, and then fall to fighting and keep it up till they were just two grotesque tangles of rags and blood and tumbled hair. Then they would rest awhile and pant and swear. While they were affectionate they always spoke of each other as "ladies," but while they were fighting "strumpet" was the mildest name they could think of--and they could only make that do by tacking some sounding profanity to it. In their last fight, which was toward midnight, one of them bit off the other's finger, and then the officer interfered and put the "Greaser" into the "dark cell" to answer for it because the woman that did it laid it on him, and the other woman did not deny it because, as she said afterward, she "wanted another crack at the huzzy when her finger quit hurting," and so she did not want her removed. By this time those two women had mutilated each other's clothes to that extent that there was not sufficient left to cover their nakedness. I found that one of these creatures had spent nine years in the county jail, and that the other one had spent about four or five years in the same place. They had done it from choice. As soon as they were discharged from captivity they would go straight and get drunk, and then steal some trifling thing while an officer was observing them. That would entitle them to another two, months in jail, and there they would occupy clean, airy apartments, and have good food in plenty, and being at no expense at all, they, could make shirts for the clothiers at half a dollar apiece and thus keep themselves in smoking tobacco and such other luxuries as they wanted. When the two months were up they would go just as straight as they could walk to Mother Leonard's and get drunk; and from there to Kearney street and steal something; and thence to this city prison, and next day back to the old quarters in the county jail again. One of them had really kept this up for nine years and the other four or five, and both said they meant to end their days in that prison. **-- [**The former of the two did.--Ed. Men.]--Finally, both these creatures fell

Mark Twain

upon me while I was dozing with my head against their grating, and battered me considerably, because they discovered that I was a Chinaman, and they said I was "a bloody interlopin' loafer come from the devil's own country to take the bread out of dacent people's mouths and put down the wages for work whin it was all a Christian could do to kape body and sowl together as it was." "Loafer" means one who will not work.

AH SONG HI.

Goldsmith's Friend Abroad Again

LETTER VI

SAN FRANCISCO, 18--DEAR CHING-FOO: To continue--the two women became reconciled to each other again through the common bond of interest and sympathy created between them by pounding me in partnership, and when they had finished me they fell to embracing each other again and swearing more eternal affection like that which had subsisted between them all the evening, barring occasional interruptions. They agreed to swear the finger-biting on the Greaser in open court, and get him sent to the penitentiary for the crime of mayhem.

Another of our company was a boy of fourteen who had been watched for some time by officers and teachers, and repeatedly detected in enticing young girls from the public schools to the lodgings of gentlemen down town. He had been furnished with lures in the form of pictures and books of a peculiar kind, and these he had distributed among his clients. There were likenesses of fifteen of these young girls on exhibition (only to prominent citizens and persons in authority, it was said, though most people came to get a sight) at the police headquarters, but no punishment at all was to be inflicted on the poor little misses. The boy was afterward sent into captivity at the House of Correction for some months, and there was a strong disposition to punish the gentlemen who had employed the boy to entice the girls, but as that could not be done without making public the names of those gentlemen and thus injuring them socially, the idea was finally given up.

There was also in our cell that night a photographer (a kind of artist who makes likenesses of people with a machine), who had been for some time patching the pictured heads of well-known and respectable young ladies to the nude, pictured bodies of another class of women; then from this patched creation he would make photographs and sell them privately at high prices to rowdies and blackguards, averring that these, the best young ladies of the city, had hired him to take their likenesses in that unclad condition. What a lecture the police judge read that photographer when he was convicted! He told him his crime was little less than an outrage. He abused that photographer till he almost made him sink through the floor, and then he fined him a hundred dollars. And he told him he might consider himself lucky that he didn't fine him a hundred and twenty-five dollars. They are awfully severe on crime here.

About two or two and a half hours after midnight, of that first experience of mine in the city prison, such of us as were dozing were awakened by a noise of beating and dragging and groaning, and in a little while a man was pushed into our den with a "There, d---n you, soak there a spell!"--and then the gate was closed and the officers went away again. The man who was thrust among us fell limp and helpless by the grating, but as nobody could reach him with a kick without the trouble of hitching along toward him or getting fairly up to deliver it, our people only grumbled at him, and cursed him, and called him insulting names--for misery and hardship do not make their victims gentle or charitable toward each other. But as he neither tried humbly to conciliate our people nor swore back at them, his unnatural conduct created surprise, and several of the party crawled to him where he lay in the dim light that came through the grating, and examined into his case. His head was very bloody and his wits were gone. After about an hour, he sat up and stared around; then his eyes grew more natural and he began to tell how that he was going along with a bag on his shoulder and a brace of policemen ordered him to stop, which he did not do--was chased and caught, beaten ferociously about the head on the way to the prison and after arrival there, and finally I thrown into our den like a dog.

And in a few seconds he sank down again and grew flighty of speech. One of our people was at last penetrated with something vaguely akin to compassion, may be, for he looked out through the gratings at the guardian officer, pacing to and fro, and said:

"Say, Mickey, this shrimp's goin' to die."

"Stop your noise!" was all the answer he got. But presently our man tried it again. He drew himself to the gratings, grasping them with his hands, and looking out through them, sat waiting till the officer was passing once more, and then said:

"Sweetness, you'd better mind your eye, now, because you beats have killed this cuss. You've busted his head and he'll pass in his checks before sun-up. You better go for a doctor, now, you bet you had."

The officer delivered a sudden rap on our man's knuckles with his club, that sent him scampering and howling among the sleeping forms on the flag-stones, and an answering burst of laughter came from the half dozen policemen idling about the railed desk in the middle of the dungeon.

But there was a putting of heads together out there presently, and a conversing in low voices, which seemed to show that our man's talk had made an impression; and presently an officer went away in a hurry, and shortly came back with a person who entered our cell and felt the bruised man's pulse and threw the glare of a lantern on his drawn face, striped with blood, and his glassy eyes, fixed and vacant. The doctor examined the man's broken head also, and presently said:

"If you'd called me an hour ago I might have saved this man, may be too late now."

Then he walked out into the dungeon and the officers surrounded him, and they kept up a low and earnest buzzing of conversation for fifteen minutes, I should think, and then the doctor took his departure from the prison. Several of the officers now came in and worked a little with the wounded man, but toward daylight he died.

It was the longest, longest night! And when the daylight came filtering reluctantly into the dungeon at last, it was the grayest, dreariest, saddest daylight! And yet, when an officer by and by turned off the sickly yellow gas flame, and immediately the gray of dawn became fresh and white, there was a lifting of my spirits that acknowledged and believed that the night was gone, and straightway I fell to stretching my sore limbs, and looking about me with a grateful sense of relief and a returning interest in life. About me lay the evidences that what seemed now a feverish dream and a nightmare was the memory of a reality instead. For on the boards lay four frowsy, ragged, bearded vagabonds, snoring --one turned end-for-end and resting an unclean foot, in a ruined stocking, on the hairy breast of a neighbour; the young boy was uneasy, and lay moaning in his sleep; other forms lay half revealed and half concealed about the floor; in the furthest corner the gray light fell upon a sheet, whose elevations and depressions indicated the places of the dead man's face and feet and folded hands; and through the dividing bars one could discern the almost nude forms of the two exiles from the county jail twined together in a drunken embrace, and sodden with sleep.

By and by all the animals in all the cages awoke, and stretched themselves, and exchanged a few cuffs and curses, and then began to clamour for breakfast. Breakfast was brought in at last--bread and beefsteak on tin plates, and black coffee in tin cups, and no grabbing allowed. And after several dreary hours of waiting, after this, we were all marched out into the dungeon and joined there by all manner of vagrants and vagabonds, of all shades and colours and nationalities, from the other cells and cages of the place; and pretty soon our whole menagerie was marched up-stairs and locked fast behind a high railing in a dirty room with a dirty audience in it. And this audience stared at us, and at a man seated on high behind what they call a pulpit in this country, and at some clerks and other officials seated below him--and waited. This was the police court.

The court opened. Pretty soon I was compelled to notice that a culprit's nationality made for or against him in this court. Overwhelming proofs were necessary to convict an Irishman of crime, and even then his punishment amounted to little; Frenchmen, Spaniards, and Italians had strict and unprejudiced justice meted out to them, in exact accordance with the evidence; negroes were promptly punished, when there was the slightest preponderance of testimony against them; but Chinamen were punished always, apparently. Now this gave me some uneasiness, I confess. I knew that this state of things must of necessity be accidental, because in this country all men were free and equal, and one person could not take to himself an advantage not accorded to all other individuals. I knew that, and yet in spite of it I was uneasy.

And I grew still more uneasy, when I found that any succored and befriended refugee from Ireland or elsewhere could stand up before that judge and swear, away the life or liberty or character of a refugee from China; but that by the law of the land the Chinaman could not testify against the Irishman. I was really and truly uneasy, but still my faith in the universal liberty that America accords and defends, and my deep veneration for the land that offered all distressed outcasts a home and protection, was strong within me, and I said to myself that it would all come out right yet.

AH SONG HI.

Goldsmith's Friend Abroad Again

Mark Twain

LETTER VII

SAN FRANCISCO, 18--. DEAR CHING FOO: I was glad enough when my case came up. An hour's experience had made me as tired of the police court as of the dungeon. I was not uneasy about the result of the trial, but on the contrary felt that as soon as the large auditory of Americans present should hear how that the rowdies had set the dogs on me when I was going peacefully along the street, and how, when I was all torn and bleeding, the officers arrested me and put me in jail and let the rowdies go free, the gallant hatred of oppression which is part of the very flesh and blood of every American would be stirred to its utmost, and I should be instantly set at liberty. In truth I began to fear for the other side. There in full view stood the ruffians who had misused me, and I began to fear that in the first burst of generous anger occasioned by the revealment of what they had done, they might be harshly handled, and possibly even banished the country as having dishonoured her and being no longer worthy to remain upon her sacred soil.

The official interpreter of the court asked my name, and then spoke it aloud so that all could hear. Supposing that all was now ready, I cleared my throat and began--in Chinese, because of my imperfect English:

"Hear, O high and mighty mandarin, and believe! As I went about my peaceful business in the street, behold certain men set a dog on me, and--

"Silence!"

It was the judge that spoke. The interpreter whispered to me that I must keep perfectly still. He said that no statement would be received from me--I must only talk through my lawyer.

I had no lawyer. In the early morning a police court lawyer (termed, in the higher circles of society, a "shyster") had come into our den in the prison and offered his services to me, but I had been obliged to go without them because I could not pay in advance or give security. I told the interpreter how the matter stood. He said I must take my chances on the witnesses then. I glanced around, and my failing confidence revived.

"Call those four Chinamen yonder," I said. "They saw it all. I remember their faces perfectly. They will prove that the white men set the dog on me when I was not harming them."

"That won't work," said he. "In this country white men can testify against Chinamen all they want to, but Chinamen ain't allowed to testify against white men!"

What a chill went through me! And then I felt the indignant blood rise to my cheek at this libel upon the Home of the Oppressed, where all men are free and equal--perfectly equal--perfectly free and perfectly equal. I despised this Chinese-speaking Spaniard for his mean slander of the land that was sheltering and feeding him. I sorely wanted to sear his eyes with that sentence from the great and good American Declaration of Independence which we have copied in letters of gold in China and keep hung up over our family altars and in our temples--I mean the one about all men being created free and equal.

But woe is me, Ching Foo, the man was right. He was right, after all. There were my witnesses, but I could not use them. But now came a new hope. I saw my white friend come in, and I felt that he had come there purposely to help me. I may almost say I knew it. So I grew easier. He passed near enough to me to say under his breath, "Don't be afraid," and then I had no more fear. But presently the rowdies recognised him and began to scowl at him in no friendly way, and to make threatening signs at him. The two officers that arrested me fixed their eyes steadily on his; he bore it well, but gave in presently, and dropped his eyes. They still gazed at his eyebrows, and every time he raised his eyes he encountered their winkless stare--until after a minute or two he ceased to lift his head at all. The judge had been giving some instructions privately to some one for a little while, but now he was ready to resume business. Then the trial so unspeakably important to me, and freighted with such prodigious consequence to my wife and children, began, progressed, ended, was recorded in the books, noted down by the newspaper reporters, and forgotten by everybody but me--all in the little space of two minutes!

"Ah Song Hi, Chinaman. Officers O'Flannigan and O'Flaherty, witnesses. Come forward, Officer O'Flannigan."

OFFICER--"He was making a disturbance in Kearny street."

JUDGE--"Any witnesses on the other side?" No response. The white friend raised his eyes encountered Officer O'Flaherty's--blushed a little--got up and left the courtroom, avoiding all glances and not taking his own from the floor.

JUDGE--"Give him five dollars or ten days."

In my desolation there was a glad surprise in the words; but it passed away when I found that he only meant that I was to be fined five dollars or imprisoned ten days longer in default of it.

There were twelve or fifteen Chinamen in our crowd of prisoners, charged with all manner of little thefts and misdemeanors, and their cases were quickly disposed of, as a general thing. When the charge came from a policeman or other white man, he made his statement and that was the end of it, unless the Chinaman's lawyer could find some white person to testify in his client's behalf, for, neither the accused Chinaman nor his countrymen being allowed to say anything, the statement of the officers or other white person was amply sufficient to convict. So, as I said, the Chinamen's cases were quickly disposed of, and fines and imprisonment promptly distributed among them. In one or two of the cases the charges against Chinamen were brought by Chinamen themselves, and in those cases Chinamen testified against Chinamen, through the interpreter; but the fixed rule of the court being that the preponderance of testimony in such cases should determine the prisoner's guilt or innocence, and there being nothing very binding about an oath administered to the lower orders of our people without the ancient solemnity of cutting off a chicken's head and burning some yellow paper at the same time, the interested parties naturally drum up a cloud of witnesses who are cheerfully willing to give evidence without ever knowing anything about the matter in hand. The judge has a custom of rattling through with as much of this testimony as his patience will stand, and then shutting off the rest and striking an average.

By noon all the business of the court was finished, and then several of us who had not fared well were remanded to prison; the judge went home; the lawyers, and officers, and spectators departed their several ways, and left the uncomely court-room to silence, solitude, and Stiggers, the newspaper reporter, which latter would now write up his items (said an ancient Chinaman to me), in the which he would praise all the policemen indiscriminately and abuse the Chinamen and dead people.

AH SONG HI.

1601

By: Mark Twain

1891

CONVERSATION

AS IT WAS BY THE SOCIAL FIRESIDE

IN THE TIME OF THE TUDORS

1601

Mark Twain

INTRODUCTION

"Born irreverent," scrawled Mark Twain on a scratch pad, "--like all other people I have ever known or heard of--I am hoping to remain so while there are any reverent irreverences left to make fun of." --[Holograph manuscript of Samuel L. Clemens, in the collection of the F. J. Meine]

Mark Twain was just as irreverent as he dared be, and 1601 reveals his richest expression of sovereign contempt for overstuffed language, genteel literature, and conventional idiocies. Later, when a magazine editor apostrophized, "O that we had a Rabelais!" Mark impishly and anonymously--submitted 1601; and that same editor, a praiser of Rabelais, scathingly abused it and the sender. In this episode, as in many others, Mark Twain, the "bad boy" of American literature, revealed his huge delight in blasting the shams of contemporary hypocrisy. Too, there was always the spirit of Tom Sawyer deviltry in Mark's make-up that prompted him, as he himself boasted, to see how much holy indignation he could stir up in the world.

WHO WROTE 1601?

The correct and complete title of 1601, as first issued, was: [Date, 1601.] 'Conversation, as it was by the Social Fireside, in the Time of the Tudors.' For many years after its anonymous first issue in 1880, its authorship was variously conjectured and widely disputed. In Boston, William T. Ball, one of the leading theatrical critics during the late 90's, asserted that it was originally written by an English actor (name not divulged) who gave it to him. Ball's original, it was said, looked like a newspaper strip in the way it was printed, and may indeed have been a proof pulled in some newspaper office. In St. Louis, William Marion Reedy, editor of the St. Louis Mirror, had seen this famous tour de force circulated in the early 80's in galley-proof form; he first learned from Eugene Field that it was from the pen of Mark Twain.

"Many people," said Reedy, "thought the thing was done by Field and attributed, as a joke, to Mark Twain. Field had a perfect genius for that sort of thing, as many extant specimens attest, and for that sort of practical joke; but to my thinking the humor of the piece is too mellow --not hard and bright and bitter--to be Eugene Field's." Reedy's opinion hits off the fundamental difference between these two great humorists; one half suspects that Reedy was thinking of Field's French Crisis.

But Twain first claimed his bantling from the fog of anonymity in 1906, in a letter addressed to Mr. Charles Orr, librarian of Case Library, Cleveland. Said Clemens, in the course of his letter, dated July 30, 1906, from Dublin, New Hampshire:

"The title of the piece is 1601. The piece is a supposititious conversation which takes place in Queen Elizabeth's closet in that year, between the Queen, Ben Jonson, Beaumont, Sir Walter Raleigh, the Duchess of Bilgewater, and one or two others, and is not, as John Hay mistakenly supposes, a serious effort to bring back our literature and philosophy to the sober and chaste Elizabeth's time; if there is a decent word findable in it, it is because I overlooked it. I hasten to assure you that it is not printed in my published writings."

TWITTING THE REV. JOSEPH TWICHELL

The circumstances of how 1601 came to be written have since been officially revealed by Albert Bigelow Paine in 'Mark Twain, A Bibliography' (1912), and in the publication of Mark Twain's Notebook (1935).

1601 was written during the summer of 1876 when the Clemens family had retreated to Quarry Farm in Elmira County, New York. Here Mrs. Clemens enjoyed relief from social obligations, the children romped over the countryside, and Mark retired to his octagonal study, which, perched high on the hill, looked out upon the valley below. It was in the famous summer of 1876, too, that Mark was putting the finishing touches to Tom Sawyer. Before the close of the same year he had already begun work on 'The Adventures of Huckleberry Finn', published in 1885. It is interesting to note the use of the title, the "Duke of Bilgewater," in Huck Finn when the "Duchess of Bilgewater" had already made her appearance in 1601. Sandwiched between his two great masterpieces, Tom Sawyer and Huck Finn, the writing of 1601 was indeed a strange interlude.

During this prolific period Mark wrote many minor items, most of them rejected by Howells, and read extensively in one of his favorite books, Pepys' Diary. Like many another writer Mark was captivated by Pepys' style and spirit, and "he determined," says Albert Bigelow Paine in his 'Mark Twain, A Biography', "to try his hand on an imaginary record of conversation and court manners of a bygone day, written in the phrase of the period. The result was 'Fireside Conversation in the Time of Queen Elizabeth', or as he later called it, '1601'. The 'conversation' recorded by a supposed Pepys of that period, was written with all the outspoken coarseness and nakedness of that rank day, when fireside sociabilities were limited only to the loosened fancy, vocabulary, and physical performance, and not by any bounds of convention."

"It was written as a letter," continues Paine, "to that robust divine, Rev. Joseph Twichell, who, unlike Howells, had no scruples about Mark's 'Elizabethan breadth of parlance.'"

The Rev. Joseph Twichell, Mark's most intimate friend for over forty years, was pastor of the Asylum Hill Congregational Church of Hartford, which Mark facetiously called the "Church of the Holy Speculators," because of its wealthy parishioners. Here Mark had first met "Joe" at a social, and their meeting ripened into a glorious, life long friendship. Twichell was a man of about Mark's own age, a profound scholar, a devout Christian, "yet a man with an exuberant sense of humor, and a profound understanding of the frailties of mankind." The Rev. Mr. Twichell performed the marriage ceremony for Mark Twain and solemnized the births of his children; "Joe," his friend, counseled him on literary as well as personal matters for the remainder of Mark's life. It is important to catch this brief glimpse of the man for whom this masterpiece was written, for without it one can not fully understand the spirit in which 1601 was written, or the keen enjoyment which Mark and "Joe" derived from it.

"SAVE ME ONE."

The story of the first issue of 1601 is one of finesse, state diplomacy, and surreptitious printing.

The Rev. "Joe" Twichell, for whose delectation the piece had been written, apparently had pocketed the document for four long years. Then, in 1880, it came into the hands of John Hay, later Secretary of State, presumably sent to him by Mark Twain. Hay pronounced the sketch a masterpiece, and wrote immediately to his old Cleveland friend, Alexander Gunn, prince of connoisseurs in art and literature. The following correspondence reveals the fine diplomacy which made the name of John Hay known throughout the world.

DEPARTMENT OF STATE Washington. June 21, 1880

Dear Gunn:

Are you in Cleveland for all this week? If you will say yes by return mail, I have a masterpiece to submit to your consideration which is only in my hands for a few days.

Yours, very much worritted by the depravity of Christendom,

Hay

The second letter discloses Hay's own high opinion of the effort and his deep concern for its safety.

June 24, 1880

My dear Gunn:

Here it is. It was written by Mark Twain in a serious effort to bring back our literature and philosophy to the sober and chaste Elizabethan standard. But the taste of the present day is too corrupt for anything so classic. He has not yet been able even to find a publisher. The Globe has not yet recovered from Downey's inroad, and they won't touch it.

I send it to you as one of the few lingering relics of that race of appreciative critics, who know a good thing when they see it.

Read it with reverence and gratitude and send it back to me; for Mark is impatient to see once more his wandering offspring.

Yours,

Hay.

In his third letter one can almost hear Hay's chuckle in the certainty that his diplomatic, if somewhat wicked, suggestion would bear fruit.

Washington, D. C . July 7, 1880

My dear Gunn:

I have your letter, and the proposition which you make to pull a few proofs of the masterpiece is highly attractive, and of course highly immoral. I cannot properly consent to it, and I am afraid the great many would think I was taking an unfair advantage of his confidence. Please send back the document as soon as you can, and if, in spite of my prohibition, you take these proofs, save me one.

Very truly yours,

John Hay.

Thus was this Elizabethan dialogue poured into the moulds of cold type. According to Merle Johnson, Mark Twain's bibliographer, it was issued in pamphlet form, without wrappers or covers; there were 8 pages of text and the pamphlet measured 7 by 8 1/2 inches. Only four copies are believed to have been printed, one for Hay, one for Gunn, and two for Twain.

"In the matter of humor," wrote Clemens, referring to Hay's delicious notes, "what an unsurpassable touch John Hay had!"

HUMOR AT WEST POINT

The first printing of 1601 in actual book form was "Donne at ye Academie Press," in 1882, West Point, New York, under the supervision of Lieut. C. E. S. Wood, then adjutant of the U. S. Military Academy.

In 1882 Mark Twain and Joe Twichell visited their friend Lieut. Wood at West Point, where they learned that Wood, as Adjutant, had under his control a small printing establishment. On Mark's return to Hartford, Wood received a letter asking if he would do Mark a great favor by printing something he had written, which he did not care to entrust to the ordinary printer. Wood replied that he would be glad to oblige. On April 3, 1882, Mark sent the manuscript:

"I enclose the original of 1603 [sic] as you suggest. I am afraid there are errors in it, also, heedlessness in antiquated spelling--e's stuck on often at end of words where they are not strickly necessary, etc..... I would go through the manuscript but I am too much driven just now, and it is not important anyway. I wish you would do me the kindness to make any and all corrections that suggest themselves to you.

    "Sincerely yours,

      "S. L. Clemens."

Charles Erskine Scott Wood recalled in a foreword, which he wrote for the limited edition of 1601 issued by the Grabhorn Press, how he felt when he first saw the original manuscript. "When I read it," writes Wood, "I felt that the character of it would be carried a little better by a printing which pretended to the eye that it was contemporaneous with the pretended 'conversation.'

"I wrote Mark that for literary effect I thought there should be a species of forgery, though of course there was no effort to actually deceive a scholar. Mark answered that I might do as I liked;--that his only object was to secure a number of copies, as the demand for it was becoming burdensome, but he would be very grateful for any interest I brought to the doing.

"Well, Tucker [foreman of the printing shop] and I soaked some handmade linen paper in weak coffee, put it as a wet bundle into a warm room to mildew, dried it to a dampness approved by Tucker and he printed the 'copy' on a hand press.   I had special punches cut for such Elizabethan abbreviations as the a, e, o and u, when followed by m or n--and for the (commonly and stupidly pronounced ye).

"The only editing I did was as to the spelling and a few old English words introduced. The spelling, if I remember correctly, is mine, but the text is exactly as written by Mark. I wrote asking his view of making the spelling of the period and he was enthusiastic--telling me to do whatever I thought best and he was greatly pleased with the result."

Thus was printed in a de luxe edition of fifty copies the most curious masterpiece of American humor, at one of America's most dignified institutions, the United States Military Academy at West Point.

"1601 was so be-praised by the archaeological scholars of a quarter of a century ago," wrote Clemens in his letter to Charles Orr, "that I was rather inordinately vain of it. At that time it had been privately printed in several countries, among them Japan. A sumptuous edition on large paper, rough-edged, was made by Lieut. C. E. S. Wood at West Point --an edition of 50 copies--and distributed among popes and kings and such people. In England copies of that issue were worth twenty guineas when I was there six years ago, and none to be had."

FROM THE DEPTHS

Mark Twain's irreverence should not be misinterpreted: it was an irreverence which bubbled up from a deep, passionate insight into the well-springs of human nature.   In 1601, as in 'The Man That Corrupted Hadleyburg,' and in 'The Mysterious Stranger,' he tore the masks off human beings and left them cringing before the public view. With the deftness of a master surgeon Clemens dealt with human emotions and delighted in exposing human nature in the raw.

The spirit and the language of the Fireside Conversation were rooted deep in Mark Twain's nature and in his life, as C. E. S. Wood, who printed 1601 at West Point, has pertinently observed,

"If I made a guess as to the intellectual ferment out of which 1601 rose I would say that Mark's intellectual structure and subconscious graining was from Anglo-Saxons as primitive as the common man of the Tudor period. He came from the banks of the Mississippi--from the flatboatmen, pilots, roustabouts, farmers and village folk of a rude, primitive people--as Lincoln did.

"He was finished in the mining camps of the West among stage drivers, gamblers and the men of '49. The simple roughness of a frontier people was in his blood and brain.

"Words vulgar and offensive to other ears were a common language to him. Anyone who ever knew Mark heard him use them freely, forcibly, picturesquely in his unrestrained conversation. Such language is forcible as all primitive words are. Refinement seems to make for weakness--or let us say a cutting edge--but the old vulgar monosyllabic words bit like the blow of a pioneer's ax--and Mark was like that. Then I think 1601 came out of Mark's instinctive humor, satire and hatred of puritanism. But there is more than this; with all its humor there is a sense of real delight in what may be called obscenity for its own sake. Whitman and the Bible are no more obscene than Nature herself--no more obscene than a manure pile, out of which come roses and cherries. Every word used in 1601 was used by our own rude pioneers as a part of their vocabulary--and no word was ever invented by man with obscene intent, but only as language to express his meaning. No act of nature is obscene in itself--but when such words and acts are dragged in for an ulterior purpose they become offensive, as everything out of place is offensive. I think he delighted, too, in shocking--giving resounding slaps on what Chaucer would quite simply call 'the bare erse.'"

Quite aside from this Chaucerian "erse" slapping, Clemens had also a semi-serious purpose, that of reproducing a past time as he saw it in Shakespeare, Dekker, Jonson, and other writers of the Elizabethan era. Fireside Conversation was an exercise in scholarship illumined by a keen sense of character. It was made especially effective by the artistic arrangement of widely-gathered material into a compressed picture of a phase of the manners and even the minds of the men and women "in the spacious times of great Elizabeth."

Mark Twain made of 1601 a very smart and fascinating performance, carried over almost to grotesqueness just to show it was not done for mere delight in the frank naturalism of the functions with which it deals. That Mark Twain had made considerable study of this frankness is apparent from chapter four of 'A Yankee At King Arthur's Court,' where he refers to the conversation at the famous Round Table thus:

"Many of the terms used in the most matter-of-fact way by this great assemblage of the first ladies and gentlemen of the land would have made a Comanche blush. Indelicacy is too mild a term to convey the idea. However, I had read Tom Jones and Roderick Random and other books of that kind and knew that the highest and first ladies and gentlemen in England had remained little or no cleaner in their talk, and in the morals and conduct which such talk implies, clear up to one hundred years ago; in fact clear into our own nineteenth century--in which century, broadly speaking, the earliest samples of the real lady and the real gentleman discoverable in English history,--or in European history, for that matter--may be said to have made their appearance. Suppose Sir Walter [Scott] instead of putting the conversation into the mouths of his characters, had allowed the characters to speak for themselves? We should have had talk from Rebecca and Ivanhoe and the soft lady Rowena which would embarrass a tramp in our day. However, to the unconsciously indelicate all things are delicate."

Mark Twain's interest in history and in the depiction of historical periods and characters is revealed through his fondness for historical reading in preference to fiction, and through his other historical writings. Even in the hilarious, youthful days in San Francisco, Paine reports that "Clemens, however, was never quite ready for sleep. Then, as ever, he would prop himself up in bed, light his pipe, and lose himself in English or French history until his sleep conquered." Paine tells us, too, that Lecky's 'European Morals' was an old favorite.

The notes to 'The Prince and the Pauper' show again how carefully Clemens examined his historical background, and his interest in these materials. Some of the more important sources are noted: Hume's 'History of England',

Timbs' 'Curiosities of London', J. Hammond Trumbull's 'Blue Laws, True and False'. Apparently Mark Twain relished it, for as Bernard DeVoto points out, "The book is always Mark Twain. Its parodies of Tudor speech lapse sometimes into a callow satisfaction in that idiom--Mark hugely enjoys his nathlesses and beshrews and marrys." The writing of 1601 foreshadows his fondness for this treatment.

"Do you suppose the liberties and the Brawn of These States have to do only with delicate lady-words? with gloved gentleman words" Walt Whitman, 'An American Primer'.

Although 1601 was not matched by any similar sketch in his published works, it was representative of Mark Twain the man. He was no emaciated literary tea-tosser. Bronzed and weatherbeaten son of the West, Mark was a man's man, and that significant fact is emphasized by the several phases of Mark's rich life as steamboat pilot, printer, miner, and frontier journalist.

On the Virginia City Enterprise Mark learned from editor R. M. Daggett that "when it was necessary to call a man names, there were no expletives too long or too expressive to be hurled in rapid succession to emphasize the utter want of character of the man assailed.... There were typesetters there who could hurl anathemas at bad copy which would have frightened a Bengal tiger. The news editor could damn a mutilated dispatch in twenty-four languages."

In San Francisco in the sizzling sixties we catch a glimpse of Mark Twain and his buddy, Steve Gillis, pausing in doorways to sing "The Doleful Ballad of the Neglected Lover," an old piece of uncollected erotica. One morning, when a dog began to howl, Steve awoke "to find his room-mate standing in the door that opened out into a back garden, holding a big revolver, his hand shaking with cold and excitement," relates Paine in his Biography.

"'Come here, Steve,' he said. 'I'm so chilled through I can't get a bead on him.'

"'Sam,' said Steve, 'don't shoot him. Just swear at him. You can easily kill him at any range with your profanity.'

"Steve Gillis declares that Mark Twain let go such a scorching, singeing blast that the brute's owner sold him the next day for a Mexican hairless dog."

Nor did Mark's "geysers of profanity" cease spouting after these gay and youthful days in San Francisco. With Clemens it may truly be said that profanity was an art--a pyrotechnic art that entertained nations.

"It was my duty to keep buttons on his shirts," recalled Katy Leary, life-long housekeeper and friend in the Clemens menage, "and he'd swear something terrible if I didn't. If he found a shirt in his drawer without a button on, he'd take every single shirt out of that drawer and throw them right out of the window, rain or shine--out of the bathroom window they'd go. I used to look out every morning to see the snowflakes--anything white. Out they'd fly.... Oh! he'd swear at anything when he was on a rampage. He'd swear at his razor if it didn't cut right, and Mrs. Clemens used to send me around to the bathroom door sometimes to knock and ask him what was the matter. Well, I'd go and knock; I'd say, 'Mrs. Clemens wants to know what's the matter.' And then he'd say to me (kind of low) in a whisper like, 'Did she hear me Katy?' 'Yes,' I'd say, 'every word.' Oh, well, he was ashamed then, he was afraid of getting scolded for swearing like that, because Mrs. Clemens hated swearing." But his swearing never seemed really bad to Katy Leary, "It was sort of funny, and a part of him, somehow," she said. "Sort of amusing it was--and gay--not like real swearing, 'cause he swore like an angel."

In his later years at Stormfield Mark loved to play his favorite billiards. "It was sometimes a wonderful and fearsome thing to watch Mr. Clemens play billiards," relates Elizabeth Wallace. "He loved the game, and he loved to win, but he occasionally made a very bad stroke, and then the varied, picturesque, and unorthodox vocabulary, acquired in his more youthful years, was the only thing that gave him comfort. Gently, slowly, with no profane inflexions of voice, but irresistibly as though they had the headwaters of the Mississippi for their source, came this stream of unholy adjectives and choice expletives."

Mark's vocabulary ran the whole gamut of life itself. In Paris, in his appearance in 1879 before the Stomach Club, a jolly lot of gay wags, Mark's address, reports Paine, "obtained a wide celebrity among the clubs of the world, though no line of it, not even its title, has ever found its way into published literature." It is rumored to have been called "Some Remarks on the Science of Onanism."

In Berlin, Mark asked Henry W. Fisher to accompany him on an exploration of the Berlin Royal Library, where the librarian, having learned that Clemens had been the Kaiser's guest at dinner, opened the secret treasure chests for the famous visitor. One of these guarded treasures was a volume of grossly indecent verses by Voltaire, addressed to Frederick the Great. "Too much is enough," Mark is reported to have said, when Fisher translated some of the verses, "I would blush to remember any of these stanzas except to tell Krafft-Ebing about them when I get to Vienna." When Fisher had finished copying a verse for him Mark put it into his pocket, saying, "Livy [Mark's wife, Olivia] is so busy mispronouncing German these days she can't even attempt to get at this."

In his letters, too, Howells observed, "He had the Southwestern, the Lincolnian, the Elizabethan breadth of parlance, which I suppose one ought not to call coarse without calling one's self prudish; and I was often hiding away in discreet holes and corners the letters in which he had loosed his bold fancy to stoop on rank suggestion; I could not bear to burn them, and I could not, after the first reading, quite bear to look at them. I shall best give my feeling on this point by saying that in it he was Shakespearean."

"With a nigger squat on her safety-valve" John Hay, Pike County Ballads.

"Is there any other explanation," asks Van Wyck Brooks, "'of his Elizabethan breadth of parlance?' Mr. Howells confesses that he sometimes blushed over Mark Twain's letters, that there were some which, to the very day when he wrote his eulogy on his dead friend, he could not bear to reread. Perhaps if he had not so insisted, in former years, while going over Mark Twain's proofs, upon 'having that swearing out in an instant,' he would never had had cause to suffer from his having 'loosed his bold fancy to stoop on rank suggestion.' Mark Twain's verbal Rabelaisianism was obviously the expression of that vital sap which, not having been permitted to inform his work, had been driven inward and left thereto ferment. No wonder he was always indulging in orgies of forbidden words. Consider the famous book, 1601, that fireside conversation in the time of Queen Elizabeth: is there any obsolete verbal indecency in the English language that Mark Twain has not painstakingly resurrected and assembled there? He, whose blood was in constant ferment and who could not contain within the narrow bonds that had been set for him the roitous exuberance of his nature, had to have an escape-valve, and he poured through it a fetid stream of meaningless obscenity--the waste of a priceless psychic material!" Thus, Brooks lumps 1601 with Mark Twain's "bawdry," and interprets it simply as another indication of frustration.

FIGS FOR FIG LEAVES!

Of course, the writing of such a piece as 1601 raised the question of freedom of expression for the creative artist.

Although little discussed at that time, it was a question which intensely interested Mark, and for a fuller appreciation of Mark's position one must keep in mind the year in which 1601 was written, 1876. There had been nothing like it before in American literature; there had appeared no Caldwells, no Faulkners, no Hemingways. Victorian England was gushing Tennyson. In the United States polite letters was a cult of the Brahmins of Boston, with William Dean Howells at the helm of the Atlantic. Louisa May Alcott published Little Women in 1868-69, and Little Men in 1871. In 1873 Mark Twain led the van of the debunkers, scraping the gilt off the lily in the Gilded Age.

In 1880 Mark took a few pot shots at license in Art and Literature in his Tramp Abroad, "I wonder why some things are? For instance, Art is allowed as much indecent license to-day as in earlier times--but the privileges of Literature in this respect have been sharply curtailed within the past eighty or ninety years. Fielding and Smollet could portray the beastliness of their day in the beastliest language; we have plenty of foul subjects to deal with in our day, but we are not allowed to approach them very near, even with nice and guarded forms of speech. But not so with Art. The brush may still deal freely with any subject; however revolting or indelicate. It makes a body ooze sarcasm at every pore, to go about Rome and Florence and see what this last generation has been doing with the statues. These works, which had stood in innocent nakedness for ages, are all fig-leaved now. Yes, every one of them. Nobody noticed their nakedness before, perhaps; nobody can help noticing it now, the fig-leaf makes it so conspicuous. But the comical thing about it all, is, that the fig-leaf is confined to cold and pallid marble, which would be still cold and unsuggestive without this sham and ostentatious symbol of modesty, whereas warm-blooded paintings which do really need it have in no case been furnished with it.

"At the door of the Ufizzi, in Florence, one is confronted by statues of a man and a woman, noseless, battered, black with accumulated grime--they hardly suggest human beings--yet these ridiculous creatures have been thoughtfully and conscientiously fig-leaved by this fastidious generation. You enter, and proceed to that most-visited little gallery that exists in the world.... and there, against the wall, without obstructing rag or leaf, you may look your fill upon the foulest, the vilest, the obscenest picture the world possesses-- Titian's Venus. It isn't that she is naked and stretched out on a bed--no, it is the attitude of one of her arms and hand. If I ventured to describe the attitude, there would be a fine howl--but there the Venus lies, for anybody to gloat over that wants to--and there she has a right to lie, for she is a work of art, and Art has its privileges. I saw young girls stealing furtive glances at her; I saw young men gaze long and absorbedly at her; I saw aged, infirm men hang upon her charms with a pathetic interest. How I should like to describe her--just to see what a holy indignation I could stir up in the world--just to hear the unreflecting average man deliver himself about my grossness and coarseness, and all that.

"In every gallery in Europe there are hideous pictures of blood, carnage, oozing brains, putrefaction--pictures portraying intolerable suffering -- pictures alive with every conceivable horror, wrought out in dreadful detail-- and similar pictures are being put on the canvas every day and publicly exhibited--without a growl from anybody--for they are innocent, they are inoffensive, being works of art. But suppose a literary artist ventured to go into a painstaking and elaborate description of one of these grisly things--the critics would skin him alive. Well, let it go, it cannot be helped; Art retains her privileges, Literature has lost hers. Somebody else may cipher out the whys and the wherefores and the consistencies of it--I haven't got time."

Mark Twain

PROFESSOR SCENTS PORNOGRAPHY

Unfortunately, 1601 has recently been tagged by Professor Edward Wagenknecht as "the most famous piece of pornography in American literature." Like many another uninformed, Prof. W. is like the little boy who is shocked to see "naughty" words chalked on the back fence, and thinks they are pornography. The initiated, after years of wading through the mire, will recognize instantly the significant difference between filthy filth and funny "filth." Dirt for dirt's sake is something else again. Pornography, an eminent American jurist has pointed out, is distinguished by the "leer of the sensualist."

"The words which are criticised as dirty," observed justice John M. Woolsey in the United States District Court of New York, lifting the ban on Ulysses by James Joyce, "are old Saxon words known to almost all men and, I venture, to many women, and are such words as would be naturally and habitually used, I believe, by the types of folk whose life, physical and mental, Joyce is seeking to describe." Neither was there "pornographic intent," according to justice Woolsey, nor was Ulysses obscene within the legal definition of that word.

"The meaning of the word 'obscene,'" the Justice indicated, "as legally defined by the courts is: tending to stir the sex impulses or to lead to sexually impure and lustful thoughts.

"Whether a particular book would tend to excite such impulses and thoughts must be tested by the court's opinion as to its effect on a person with average sex instincts--what the French would call 'l'homme moyen sensuel'--who plays, in this branch of legal inquiry, the same role of hypothetical reagent as does the 'reasonable man' in the law of torts and 'the learned man in the art' on questions of invention in patent law."

Obviously, it is ridiculous to say that the "leer of the sensualist" lurks in the pages of Mark Twain's 1601.

DROLL STORY

"In a way," observed William Marion Reedy, "1601 is to Twain's whole works what the 'Droll Stories' are to Balzac's. It is better than the privately circulated ribaldry and vulgarity of Eugene Field; is, indeed, an essay in a sort of primordial humor such as we find in Rabelais, or in the plays of some of the lesser stars that drew their light from Shakespeare's urn. It is humor or fun such as one expects, let us say, from the peasants of Thomas Hardy, outside of Hardy's books. And, though it be filthy, it yet hath a splendor of mere animalism of good spirits... I would say it is scatalogical rather than erotic, save for one touch toward the end. Indeed, it seems more of Rabelais than of Boccaccio or Masuccio or Aretino--is brutally British rather than lasciviously latinate, as to the subjects, but sumptuous as regards the language."

Immediately upon first reading, John Hay, later Secretary of State, had proclaimed 1601 a masterpiece. Albert Bigelow Paine, Mark Twain's biographer, likewise acknowledged its greatness, when he said, "1601 is a genuine classic, as classics of that sort go. It is better than the gross obscenities of Rabelais, and perhaps in some day to come, the taste that justified Gargantua and the Decameron will give this literary refugee shelter and setting among the more conventional writing of Mark Twain. Human taste is a curious thing; delicacy is purely a matter of environment and point of view."

"It depends on who writes a thing whether it is coarse or not," wrote Clemens in his notebook in 1879. "I built a conversation which could have happened--I used words such as were used at that time--1601. I sent it anonymously to a magazine, and how the editor abused it and the sender!"

But that man was a praiser of Rabelais and had been saying, 'O that we had a Rabelais!' I judged that I could furnish him one.

"Then I took it to one of the greatest, best and most learned of Divines [Rev. Joseph H. Twichell] and read it to him. He came within an ace of killing himself with laughter (for between you and me the thing was dreadfully funny. I don't often write anything that I laugh at myself, but I can hardly think of that thing without laughing). That old Divine said it was a piece of the finest kind of literary art--and David Gray of the Buffalo Courier said it ought to be printed privately and left behind me when I died, and then my fame as a literary artist would last."

FRANKLIN J. MEINE

1601

Mark Twain

THE FIRST PRINTING
VERBATIM REPRINT

[Date, 1601.]

CONVERSATION, AS IT WAS BY THE SOCIAL FIRESIDE, IN THE TIME OF THE TUDORS.

[Mem.--The following is supposed to be an extract from the diary of the Pepys of that day, the same being Queen Elizabeth's cup-bearer. He is supposed to be of ancient and noble lineage; that he despises these literary canaille; that his soul consumes with wrath, to see the queen stooping to talk with such; and that the old man feels that his nobility is defiled by contact with Shakespeare, etc., and yet he has got to stay there till her Majesty chooses to dismiss him.]

YESTERNIGHT toke her maiste ye queene a fantasie such as she sometimes hath, and had to her closet certain that doe write playes, bokes, and such like, these being my lord Bacon, his worship Sir Walter Ralegh, Mr. Ben Jonson, and ye child Francis Beaumonte, which being but sixteen, hath yet turned his hand to ye doing of ye Lattin masters into our Englishe tong, with grete discretion and much applaus. Also came with these ye famous Shaxpur. A righte straunge mixing truly of mighty blode with mean, ye more in especial since ye queenes grace was present, as likewise these following, to wit: Ye Duchess of Bilgewater, twenty-two yeres of age;

ye Countesse of Granby, twenty-six; her doter, ye Lady Helen, fifteen; as also these two maides of honor, to-wit, ye Lady Margery Boothy, sixty-five, and ye Lady Alice Dilberry, turned seventy, she being two yeres ye queenes graces elder.

I being her maites cup-bearer, had no choice but to remaine and beholde rank forgot, and ye high holde converse wh ye low as uppon equal termes, a grete scandal did ye world heare thereof.

In ye heat of ye talk it befel yt one did breake wind, yielding an exceding mightie and distresfull stink, whereat all did laugh full sore, and then--

Ye Queene.--Verily in mine eight and sixty yeres have I not heard the fellow to this fart. Meseemeth, by ye grete sound and clamour of it, it was male; yet ye belly it did lurk behinde shoulde now fall lean and flat against ye spine of him yt hath bene delivered of so stately and so waste a bulk, where as ye guts of them yt doe quiff-splitters bear, stand comely still and rounde. Prithee let ye author confess ye offspring. Will my Lady Alice testify?

Lady Alice.--Good your grace, an' I had room for such a thundergust within mine ancient bowels, 'tis not in reason I coulde discharge ye same and live to thank God for yt He did choose handmaid so humble whereby to shew his power. Nay, 'tis not I yt have broughte forth this rich o'ermastering fog, this fragrant gloom, so pray you seeke ye further.

Ye Queene.--Mayhap ye Lady Margery hath done ye companie this favor?

Lady Margery.--So please you madam, my limbs are feeble wh ye weighte and drouth of five and sixty winters, and it behoveth yt I be tender unto them. In ye good providence of God, an' I had contained this wonder, forsoothe wolde I have gi'en 'ye whole evening of my sinking life to ye dribbling of it forth, with trembling and uneasy soul, not launched it sudden in its matchless might, taking mine own life with violence, rending my weak frame like rotten rags. It was not I, your maisty.

Ye Queene.--O' God's name, who hath favored us? Hath it come to pass yt a fart shall fart itself? Not such a one as this, I trow. Young Master Beaumont--but no; 'twould have wafted him to heaven like down of goose's boddy. 'Twas not ye little Lady Helen--nay, ne'er blush, my child; thoul't tickle thy tender maidenhedde with many a mousie-squeak before thou learnest to blow a harricane like this. Wasn't you, my learned and ingenious Jonson?

Jonson.--So fell a blast hath ne'er mine ears saluted, nor yet a stench so all-pervading and immortal. 'Twas not a novice did it, good your maisty, but one of veteran experience--else hadde he failed of confidence. In sooth it was not I.

Ye Queene.--My lord Bacon?

Lord Bacon.-Not from my leane entrailes hath this prodigy burst forth, so please your grace. Naught doth so befit ye grete as grete performance; and haply shall ye finde yt 'tis not from mediocrity this miracle hath issued.

[Tho' ye subjoct be but a fart, yet will this tedious sink of learning pondrously phillosophize. Meantime did the foul and deadly stink pervade all places to that degree, yt never smelt I ye like, yet dare I not to leave ye presence, albeit I was like to suffocate.]

Ye Queene.--What saith ye worshipful Master Shaxpur?

Shaxpur.--In the great hand of God I stand and so proclaim mine innocence. Though ye sinless hosts of heaven had foretold ye coming of this most desolating breath, proclaiming it a work of uninspired man, its quaking thunders, its firmament-clogging rottenness his own achievement in due course of nature, yet had not I believed it; but had said the pit itself hath furnished forth the stink, and heaven's artillery hath shook the globe in admiration of it.

[Then was there a silence, and each did turn him toward the worshipful Sr Walter Ralegh, that browned, embattled, bloody swashbuckler, who rising up did smile, and simpering say,]

Sr W.--Most gracious maisty, 'twas I that did it, but indeed it was so poor and frail a note, compared with such as I am wont to furnish, yt in sooth I was ashamed to call the weakling mine in so august a presence. It was nothing--less than nothing, madam--I did it but to clear my nether throat; but had I come prepared, then had I delivered something worthy. Bear with me, please your grace, till I can make amends.

[Then delivered he himself of such a godless and rock-shivering blast that all were fain to stop their ears, and following it did come so dense and foul a stink that that which went before did seem a poor and trifling thing beside it. Then saith he, feigning that he blushed and was confused, I perceive that I am weak to-day, and cannot justice do unto my powers; and sat him down as who should say, There, it is not much yet he that hath an arse to spare, let him fellow that, an' he think he can. By God, an' I were ye queene, I would e'en tip this swaggering braggart out o' the court, and let him air his grandeurs and break his intolerable wind before ye deaf and such as suffocation pleaseth.]

Then fell they to talk about ye manners and customs of many peoples, and Master Shaxpur spake of ye boke of ye sieur Michael de Montaine, wherein was mention of ye custom of widows of Perigord to wear uppon ye headdress, in sign of widowhood, a jewel in ye similitude of a man's member wilted and limber, whereat ye queene did laugh and say widows in England doe wear prickes too, but betwixt the thighs, and not wilted neither, till coition hath done that office for them. Master Shaxpur did likewise observe how yt ye sieur de Montaine hath also spoken of a certain emperor of such mighty prowess that he did take ten maidenheddes in ye compass of a single night, ye while his empress did entertain two and twenty lusty knights between her sheetes, yet was not satisfied; whereat ye merrie Countess Granby saith a ram is yet ye emperor's superior, sith he wil tup above a hundred yewes 'twixt sun and sun; and after, if he can have none more to shag, will masturbate until he hath enrich'd whole acres with his seed.

Then spake ye damned windmill, Sr Walter, of a people in ye uttermost parts of America, yt capulate not until they be five and thirty yeres of age, ye women being eight and twenty, and do it then but once in seven yeres.

Ye Queene.--How doth that like my little Lady Helen? Shall we send thee thither and preserve thy belly?

Lady Helen.--Please your highnesses grace, mine old nurse hath told me there are more ways of serving God than by locking the thighs together; yet am I willing to serve him yt way too, sith your highnesses grace hath set ye ensample.

Ye Queene.--God' wowndes a good answer, childe.

Mark Twain

Lady Alice.--Mayhap 'twill weaken when ye hair sprouts below ye navel.

Lady Helen.--Nay, it sprouted two yeres syne; I can scarce more than cover it with my hand now.

Ye Queene.--Hear Ye that, my little Beaumonte? Have ye not a little birde about ye that stirs at hearing tell of so sweete a neste?

Beaumonte.--'Tis not insensible, illustrious madam; but mousing owls and bats of low degree may not aspire to bliss so whelming and ecstatic as is found in ye downy nests of birdes of Paradise.

Ye Queene.--By ye gullet of God, 'tis a neat-turned compliment. With such a tongue as thine, lad, thou'lt spread the ivory thighs of many a willing maide in thy good time, an' thy cod-piece be as handy as thy speeche.

Then spake ye queene of how she met old Rabelais when she was turned of fifteen, and he did tell her of a man his father knew that had a double pair of bollocks, whereon a controversy followed as concerning the most just way to spell the word, ye contention running high betwixt ye learned Bacon and ye ingenious Jonson, until at last ye old Lady Margery, wearying of it all, saith, 'Gentles, what mattereth it how ye shall spell the word? I warrant Ye when ye use your bollocks ye shall not think of it; and my Lady Granby, be ye content; let the spelling be, ye shall enjoy the beating of them on your buttocks just the same, I trow. Before I had gained my fourteenth year I had learnt that them that would explore a cunt stop'd not to consider the spelling o't.'

Sr W.--In sooth, when a shift's turned up, delay is meet for naught but dalliance. Boccaccio hath a story of a priest that did beguile a maid into his cell, then knelt him in a corner to pray for grace to be rightly thankful for this tender maidenhead ye Lord had sent him; but ye abbot, spying through ye key-hole, did see a tuft of brownish hair with fair white flesh about it, wherefore when ye priest's prayer was done, his chance was gone, forasmuch as ye little maid had but ye one cunt, and that was already occupied to her content.

Then conversed they of religion, and ye mightie work ye old dead Luther did doe by ye grace of God. Then next about poetry, and Master Shaxpur did rede a part of his King Henry IV., ye which, it seemeth unto me, is not of ye value of an arsefull of ashes, yet they praised it bravely, one and all.

Ye same did rede a portion of his "Venus and Adonis," to their prodigious admiration, whereas I, being sleepy and fatigued withal, did deme it but paltry stuff, and was the more discomforted in that ye blody bucanier had got his wind again, and did turn his mind to farting with such villain zeal that presently I was like to choke once more. God damn this windy ruffian and all his breed. I wolde that hell mighte get him.

They talked about ye wonderful defense which old Sr. Nicholas Throgmorton did make for himself before ye judges in ye time of Mary; which was unlucky matter to broach, sith it fetched out ye quene with a 'Pity yt he, having so much wit, had yet not enough to save his doter's maidenhedde sound for her marriage-bed.' And ye quene did give ye damn'd Sr. Walter a look yt made hym wince--for she hath not forgot he was her own lover it yt olde day. There was silent uncomfortableness now; 'twas not a good turn for talk to take, sith if ye queene must find offense in a little harmless debauching, when pricks were stiff and cunts not loathe to take ye stiffness out of them, who of this company was sinless; behold, was not ye wife of Master Shaxpur four months gone with child when she stood uppe before ye altar? Was not her Grace of Bilgewater roger'd by four lords before she had a husband? Was not ye little Lady Helen born on her mother's wedding-day? And, beholde, were not ye Lady Alice and ye Lady Margery there, mouthing religion, whores from ye cradle?

In time came they to discourse of Cervantes, and of the new painter, Rubens, that is beginning to be heard of. Fine words and dainty-wrought phrases from the ladies now, one or two of them being, in other days, pupils of that poor ass, Lille, himself; and I marked how that Jonson and Shaxpur did fidget to discharge some venom of sarcasm, yet dared they not in the presence, the queene's grace being ye very flower of ye Euphuists herself. But behold, these be they yt, having a specialty, and admiring it in themselves, be jealous when a neighbor doth essaye it, nor can abide it in them long. Wherefore 'twas observable yt ye quene waxed uncontent; and in time labor'd grandiose speeche out of ye mouth of Lady Alice, who manifestly did mightily pride herself thereon, did quite exhauste ye quene's endurance, who listened till ye gaudy speeche was done, then lifted up her brows, and with vaste irony, mincing saith 'O shit!' Whereat they alle did laffe, but not ye Lady Alice, yt olde foolish bitche.

Now was Sr. Walter minded of a tale he once did hear ye ingenious Margrette of Navarre relate, about a maid, which being like to suffer rape by an olde archbishoppe, did smartly contrive a device to save her maidenhedde, and said to him, First, my lord, I prithee, take out thy holy tool and piss before me; which doing, lo his member felle, and would not rise again.

FOOTNOTES

To Frivolity

The historical consistency of 1601 indicates that Twain must have given the subject considerable thought. The author was careful to speak only of men who conceivably might have been in the Virgin Queen's closet and engaged in discourse with her.

THE CHARACTERS

At this time (1601) Queen Elizabeth was 68 years old. She speaks of having talked to "old Rabelais" in her youth. This might have been possible as Rabelais died in 1552, when the Queen was 19 years old.

Among those in the party were Shakespeare, at that time 37 years old; Ben Jonson, 27; and Sir Walter Raleigh, 49. Beaumont at the time was 17, not 16. He was admitted as a member of the Inner Temple in 1600, and his first translations, those from Ovid, were first published in 1602. Therefore, if one were holding strictly to the year date, neither by age nor by fame would Beaumont have been eligible to attend such a gathering of august personages in the year 1601; but the point is unimportant.

THE ELIZABETHAN WRITERS

In the Conversation Shakespeare speaks of Montaigne's Essays. These were first published in 1580 and successive editions were issued in the years following, the third volume being published in 1588. "In England Montaigne was early popular. It was long supposed that the autograph of Shakespeare in a copy of Florio's translation showed his study of the Essays. The autograph has been disputed, but divers passages, and especially one in The Tempest, show that at first or second hand the poet was acquainted with the essayist." (Encyclopedia Brittanica.)

The company at the Queen's fireside discoursed of Lilly (or Lyly), English dramatist and novelist of the Elizabethan era, whose novel, Euphues, published in two parts, 'Euphues', or the 'Anatomy of Wit' (1579) and 'Euphues and His England' (1580) was a literary sensation. It is said to have influenced literary style for more than a quarter of a century, and traces of its influence are found in Shakespeare. (Columbia Encyclopedia).

The introduction of Ben Jonson into the party was wholly appropriate, if one may call to witness some of Jonson's writings. The subject under discussion was one that Jonson was acquainted with, in The Alchemist:

Act. I, Scene I,

FACE: Believe't I will.

SUBTLE: Thy worst. I fart at thee.

DOL COMMON: Have you your wits? Why, gentlemen, for love----

Act. 2, Scene I,

SIR EPICURE MAMMON: ....and then my poets, the same that writ so subtly of the fart, whom I shall entertain still for that subject and again in Bartholomew Fair

NIGHTENGALE: (sings a ballad)

Hear for your love, and buy for your money.
A delicate ballad o' the ferret and the coney.

A preservative again' the punk's evil.
Another goose-green starch, and the devil.
A dozen of divine points, and the godly garter
The fairing of good counsel, of an ell and three-quarters.
What is't you buy?
The windmill blown down by the witche's fart,
Or Saint George, that, O! did break the dragon's heart.

GOOD OLD ENGLISH CUSTOM

That certain types of English society have not changed materially in their freedom toward breaking wind in public can be noticed in some comparatively recent literature. Frank Harris in My Life, Vol. 2, Ch. XIII, tells of Lady Marriott, wife of a judge Advocate General, being compelled to leave her own table, at which she was entertaining Sir Robert Fowler, then the Lord Mayor of London, because of the suffocating and nauseating odors there. He also tells of an instance in parliament, and of a rather brilliant bon mot spoken upon that occasion.

"While Fowler was speaking Finch-Hatton had shewn signs of restlessness; towards the end of the speech he had moved some three yards away from the Baronet. As soon as Fowler sat down Finch-Hatton sprang up holding his handkerchief to his nose:

"'Mr. Speaker,' he began, and was at once acknowledged by the Speaker, for it was a maiden speech, and as such was entitled to precedence by the courteous custom of the House, 'I know why the Right Honourable Member from the City did not conclude his speech with a proposal. The only way to conclude such a speech appropriately would be with a motion!'"

AEOLIAN CREPITATIONS

But society had apparently degenerated sadly in modern times, and even in the era of Elizabeth, for at an earlier date it was a serious--nay, capital-- offense to break wind in the presence of majesty. The Emperor Claudius, hearing that one who had suppressed the urge while paying him court had suffered greatly thereby, "intended to issue an edict, allowing to all people the liberty of giving vent at table to any distension occasioned by flatulence:"

Martial, too (Book XII, Epigram LXXVII), tells of the embarrassment of one who broke wind while praying in the Capitol,

"One day, while standing upright, addressing his prayers to Jupiter, Aethon farted in the Capitol. Men laughed, but the Father of the Gods, offended, condemned the guilty one to dine at home for three nights. Since that time, miserable Aethon, when he wishes to enter the Capitol, goes first to Paterclius' privies and farts ten or twenty times. Yet, in spite of this precautionary crepitation, he salutes Jove with constricted buttocks." Martial also (Book IV, Epigram LXXX), ridicules a woman who was subject to the habit, saying,

"Your Bassa, Fabullus, has always a child at her side, calling it her darling and her plaything; and yet--more wonder--she does not care for children. What is the reason then. Bassa is apt to fart. (For which she could blame the unsuspecting infant.)"

The tale is told, too, of a certain woman who performed an aeolian crepitation at a dinner attended by the witty Monsignieur Dupanloup, Bishop of Orleans, and that when, to cover up her lapse, she began to scrape her feet upon the floor, and to make similar noises, the Bishop said, "Do not trouble to find a rhyme, Madam!"

Nay, worthier names than those of any yet mentioned have discussed the matter. Herodotus tells of one such which was the precursor to the fall of an empire and a change of dynasty--that which Amasis discharges while on horseback, and bids the envoy of Apries, King of Egypt, catch and deliver to his royal master. Even the exact manner and posture of Amasis, author of this insult, is described.

St. Augustine (The City of God, XIV:24) cites the instance of a man who could command his rear trumpet to sound at will, which his learned commentator fortifies with the example of one who could do so in tune!

Benjamin Franklin, in his "Letter to the Royal Academy of Brussels" has canvassed suggested remedies for alleviating the stench attendant upon these discharges:

"My Prize Question therefore should be: To discover some Drug, wholesome and--not disagreeable, to be mixed with our common food, or sauces, that shall render the natural discharges of Wind from our Bodies not only inoffensive, but agreeable as Perfumes.

"That this is not a Chimerical Project & altogether impossible, may appear from these considerations. That we already have some knowledge of means capable of varying that smell. He that dines on stale Flesh, especially with much Addition of Onions, shall be able to afford a stink that no Company can tolerate; while he that has lived for some time on Vegetables only, shall have that Breath so pure as to be insensible of the most delicate Noses; and if he can manage so as to avoid the Report, he may anywhere give vent to his Griefs, unnoticed. But as there are many to whom an entire Vegetable Diet would be inconvenient, & as a little quick Lime thrown into a Jakes will correct the amazing Quantity of fetid Air arising from the vast Mass of putrid Matter contained in such Places, and render it pleasing to the Smell, who knows but that a little Powder of Lime (or some other equivalent) taken in our Food, or perhaps a Glass of Lime Water drank at Dinner, may have the same Effect on the Air produced in and issuing from our Bowels?"

One curious commentary on the text is that Elizabeth should be so fond of investigating into the authorship of the exhalation in question, when she was inordinately fond of strong and sweet perfumes; in fact, she was responsible for the tremendous increase in importations of scents into England during her reign.

"YE BOKE OF YE SIEUR MICHAEL DE MONTAINE"

There is a curious admixture of error and misunderstanding in this part of the sketch. In the first place, the story is borrowed from Montaigne, where it is told inaccurately, and then further corrupted in the telling.

It was not the good widows of Perigord who wore the phallus upon their coifs; it was the young married women, of the district near Montaigne's home, who paraded it to view upon their foreheads, as a symbol, says our essayist, "of the joy they derived therefrom." If they became widows, they reversed its position, and covered it up with the rest of their head-dress.

The "emperor" mentioned was not an emperor; he was Procolus, a native of Albengue, on the Genoese coast, who, with Bonosus, led the unsuccessful rebellion in Gaul against Emperor Probus. Even so keen a commentator as Cotton has failed to note the error.

The empress (Montaigne does not say "his empress") was Messalina, third wife of the Emperor Claudius, who was uncle of Caligula and foster-father to Nero. Furthermore, in her case the charge is that she copulated with twenty-five in a single night, and not twenty-two, as appears in the text. Montaigne is right in his statistics, if original sources are correct, whereas the author erred in transcribing the incident.

As for Proculus, it has been noted that he was associated with Bonosus, who was as renowned in the field of Bacchus as was Proculus in that of Venus (Gibbon, Decline and Fall of the Roman Empire). The feat of Proculus is told in his own words, in Vopiscus, (Hist. Augustine, p. 246) where he recounts having captured one hundred Sarmatian virgins, and unmaidened ten of them in one night, together with the happenings subsequent thereto.

Concerning Messalina, there appears to be no question but that she was a nymphomaniac, and that, while Empress of Rome, she participated in some fearful debaucheries. The question is what to believe, for much that we have heard about her is almost certainly apocryphal.

The author from whom Montaigne took his facts is the elder Pliny, who, in his Natural History, Book X, Chapter 83, says, "Other animals become sated with veneral pleasures; man hardly knows any satiety. Messalina, the wife of Claudius Caesar, thinking this a palm quite worthy of an empress, selected for the purpose of deciding the question, one of the most notorious women who followed the profession of a hired prostitute; and the empress outdid her, after continuous intercourse, night and day, at the twenty-fifth embrace."

But Pliny, notwithstanding his great attainments, was often a retailer of stale gossip, and in like case was Aurelius Victor, another writer who heaped much odium on her name. Again, there is a great hiatus in the Annals of Tacitus, a true historian, at the period covering the earlier days of the

Empress; while Suetonius, bitter as he may be, is little more than an anecdotist. Juvenal, another of her detractors, is a prejudiced witness, for he started out to satirize female vice, and naturally aimed at high places. Dio also tells of Messalina's misdeeds, but his work is under the same limitations as that of Suetonius. Furthermore, none but Pliny mentions the excess under consideration.

However, "where there is much smoke there must be a little fire," and based upon the superimposed testimony of the writers of the period, there appears little doubt but that Messalina was a nymphomaniac, that she prostituted herself in the public stews, naked, and with gilded nipples, and that she did actually marry her chief adulterer, Silius, while Claudius was absent at Ostia, and that the wedding was consummated in the presence of a concourse of witnesses. This was "the straw that broke the camel's back." Claudius hastened back to Rome, Silius was dispatched, and Messalina, lacking the will-power to destroy herself, was killed when an officer ran a sword through her abdomen, just as it appeared that Claudius was about to relent.

"THEN SPAKE YE DAMNED WINDMILL, SIR WALTER"

Raleigh is thoroughly in character here; this observation is quite in keeping with the general veracity of his account of his travels in Guiana, one of the most mendacious accounts of adventure ever told. Naturally, the scholarly researches of Westermarck have failed to discover this people; perhaps Lady Helen might best be protected among the Jibaros of Ecuador, where the men marry when approaching forty.

Ben Jonson in his Conversations observed "That Sr. W. Raughlye esteemed more of fame than of conscience."

YE VIRGIN QUEENE

Grave historians have debated for centuries the pretensions of Elizabeth to the title, "The Virgin Queen," and it is utterly impossible to dispose of the issue in a note. However, the weight of opinion appears to be in the negative. Many and great were the difficulties attending the marriage of a Protestant princess in those troublous times, and Elizabeth finally announced that she would become wedded to the English nation, and she wore a ring in token thereof until her death. However, more or less open liaisons with Essex and Leicester, as well as a host of lesser courtiers, her ardent temperament, and her imperious temper, are indications that cannot be denied in determining any estimate upon the point in question.

Ben Jonson in his Conversations with William Drummond of Hawthornden says,

"Queen Elizabeth never saw herself after she became old in a true glass; they painted her, and sometymes would vermillion her nose. She had allwayes about Christmass evens set dice that threw sixes or five, and she knew not they were other, to make her win and esteame herself fortunate. That she had a membrana on her, which made her uncapable of man, though for her delight she tried many. At the comming over of Monsieur, there was a French Chirurgion who took in hand to cut it, yett fear stayed her, and his death."

It was a subject which again intrigued Clemens when he was abroad with W. H. Fisher, whom Mark employed to "nose up" everything pertaining to Queen Elizabeth's manly character.

"'BOCCACCIO HATH A STORY"

The author does not pay any great compliment to Raleigh's memory here. There is no such tale in all Boccaccio. The nearest related incident forms the subject matter of Dineo's novel (the fourth) of the First day of the Decameron.

OLD SR. NICHOLAS THROGMORTON

The incident referred to appears to be Sir Nicholas Throgmorton's trial for complicity in the attempt to make Lady Jane Grey Queen of England, a charge of which he was acquitted. This so angered Queen Mary that she imprisoned him in the Tower, and fined the jurors from one to two thousand pounds each. Her action terrified succeeding juries, so that Sir Nicholas's brother was condemned on no stronger evidence than that which had failed to prevail before. While Sir Nicholas's defense may have been brilliant, it must be admitted that the evidence was weak. He was later released from the Tower, and under Elizabeth was one of a group of commissioners sent by that princess into Scotland, to foment trouble with Mary, Queen of Scots. When the attempt became known, Elizabeth repudiated the acts of her agents, but Sir Nicholas, having anticipated this possibility, had sufficient foresight to secure endorsement of his plan by the Council, and so outwitted Elizabeth, who was playing a two-faced role, and Cecil, one of the greatest statesmen who ever held the post of principal minister. Perhaps it was this incident to which the company referred, which might in part explain Elizabeth's rejoinder. However, he had been restored to confidence ere this, and had served as ambassador to France.

"TO SAVE HIS DOTER'S MAIDENHEDDE"

Elizabeth Throckmorton (or Throgmorton), daughter of Sir Nicholas, was one of Elizabeth's maids of honor. When it was learned that she had been debauched by Raleigh, Sir Walter was recalled from his command at sea by the Queen, and compelled to marry the girl. This was not "in that olde daie," as the text has it, for it happened only eight years before the date of this purported "conversation," when Elizabeth was sixty years old.

PARTIAL BIBLIOGRAPHY

The various printings of 1601 reveal how Mark Twain's 'Fireside Conversation' has become a part of the American printer's lore. But more important, its many printings indicate that it has become a popular bit of American folklore, particularly for men and women who have a feeling for Mark Twain. Apparently it appeals to the typographer, who devotes to it his worthy art, as well as to the job printer, who may pull a crudely printed proof. The gay procession of curious printings of 1601 is unique in the history of American printing.

Indeed, the story of the various printings of 1601 is almost legendary. In the days of the "jour." printer, so I am told, well-thumbed copies were carried from print shop to print shop. For more than a quarter century now it has been one of the chief sources of enjoyment for printers' devils; and many a young rascal has learned about life from this Fireside Conversation. It has been printed all over the country, and if report is to be believed, in foreign countries as well. Because of the many surreptitious and anonymous printings it is exceedingly difficult, if not impossible, to compile a complete bibliography. Many printings lack the name of the publisher, the printer, the place or date of printing. In many instances some of the data, through the patient questioning of fellow collectors, has been obtained and supplied.

1. [Date, 1601.] Conversation, as it was by the Social Fireside, in the Time of the Tudors.

DESCRIPTION: Pamphlet, pp. [1]-8, without wrappers or cover, measuring 7x8 inches. The title is Set in caps. and small caps.

The excessively rare first printing, printed in Cleveland, 1880, at the instance of Alexander Gunn, friend of John Hay. Only four copies are believed to have been printed, of which, it is said now, the only known copy is located in the Willard S. Morse collection.

2. Date 1601. Conversation, as it was by the Social Fireside, in the time of the Tudors.

(Mem.--The following is supposed to be an extract from the diary of the Pepys of that day, the same being cup-bearer to Queen Elizabeth. It is supposed that he is of ancient and noble lineage; that he despises these literary canaille; that his soul consumes with wrath to see the Queen stooping to talk with such; and that the old man feels his nobility defiled by contact with Shakespeare, etc., and yet he has got to stay there till Her Majesty chooses to dismiss him.)

DESCRIPTION: Title as above, verso blank; pp. [i]-xi, text; verso p. xi blank. About 8 x 10 inches, printed on handmade linen paper soaked in weak coffee, wrappers. The title is set in caps and small caps.

COLOPHON: at the foot of p. xi: Done Att Ye Academie Preffe; M DCCC LXXX II.

The privately printed West Point edition, the first printing of the text authorized by Mark Twain, of which but fifty copies were printed. The story of this printing is fully told in the Introduction.

Mark Twain

3. Conversation As It Was By The Social Fire-side In The Time Of The Tudors from Ye Diary of Ye Cupbearer to her Maisty Queen Elizabeth. [design] Imprinted by Ye Puritan Press At Ye Sign of Ye Jolly Virgin 1601.

DESCRIPTION: 2 blank leaves; p. [i] blank, p. [ii] fronds., p. [iii] title [as above], p. [iv] "Mem.", pp. 1-[25] text, I blank leaf. 4 3/4 by 6 1/4 inches, printed in a modern version of the Caxton black letter type, on M.B.M. French handmade paper. The frontispiece, a woodcut by A. E. Curtis, is a portrait of the cup-bearer. Bound in buff-grey boards, buckram back. Cover title reads, in pale red ink, Caxton type, Conversation As It Was By The Social Fire-side In The Time Of The Tudors. [The Byway Press, Cincinnati, Ohio, 1901, 120 copies.]

Probably the first published edition.

Later, in 1916, a facsimile edition of this printing was published in Chicago from plates.

IS SHAKESPEARE DEAD?

From My Autobiography

By: Mark Twain

Is Shakespeare Dead?

CHAPTER I

Scattered here and there through the stacks of unpublished manuscript which constitute this formidable Autobiography and Diary of mine, certain chapters will in some distant future be found which deal with "Claimants"— claimants historically notorious: Satan, Claimant; the Golden Calf, Claimant; the Veiled Prophet of Khorassan, Claimant; Louis XVII., Claimant; William Shakespeare, Claimant; Arthur Orton, Claimant; Mary Baker G. Eddy, Claimant—and the rest of them. Eminent Claimants, successful Claimants, defeated Claimants, royal Claimants, pleb Claimants, showy Claimants, shabby Claimants, revered Claimants, despised Claimants, twinkle starlike here and there and yonder through the mists of history and legend and tradition—and oh, all the darling tribe are clothed in mystery and romance, and we read about them with deep interest and discuss them with loving sympathy or with rancorous resentment, according to which side we hitch ourselves to. It has always been so with the human race. There was never a Claimant that couldn't get a hearing, nor one that couldn't accumulate a rapturous following, no matter how flimsy and apparently unauthentic his claim might be. Arthur Orton's claim that he was the lost Tichborne baronet come to life again was as flimsy as Mrs. Eddy's that she wrote *Science and Health* from the direct dictation of the Deity; yet in England near forty years ago Orton had a huge army of devotees and incorrigible adherents, many of whom remained stubbornly unconvinced after their fat god had been proven an impostor and jailed as a perjurer, and to-day Mrs. Eddy's following is not only immense, but is daily augmenting in numbers and enthusiasm. Orton had many fine and educated minds among his adherents, Mrs. Eddy has had the like among hers from the beginning. Her church is as well equipped in those particulars as is any other church. Claimants can always count upon a following, it doesn't matter who they are, nor what they claim, nor whether they come with documents or without. It was always so. Down out of the long-vanished past, across the abyss of the ages, if you listen you can still hear the believing multitudes shouting for Perkin Warbeck and Lambert Simnel.

A friend has sent me a new book, from England—*The Shakespeare Problem Restated*—well restated and closely reasoned; and my fifty years' interest in that matter—asleep for the last three years—is excited once more. It is an interest which was born of Delia Bacon's book—away back in that ancient day—1857, or maybe 1856. About a year later my pilot-master, Bixby, transferred me from his own steamboat to the *Pennsylvania*, and placed me under the orders and instructions of George Ealer—dead now, these many, many years. I steered for him a good many months—as was the humble duty of the pilot-apprentice: stood a daylight watch and spun the wheel under the severe superintendence and correction of the master. He was a prime chess player and an idolater of Shakespeare. He would play chess with anybody; even with me, and it cost his official dignity something to do that. Also—quite uninvited—he would read Shakespeare to me; not just casually, but by the hour, when it was his watch, and I was steering. He read well, but not profitably for me, because he constantly injected commands into the text. That broke it all up, mixed it all up, tangled it all up—to that degree, in fact, that if we were in a risky and difficult piece of river an ignorant person couldn't have told, sometimes, which observations were Shakespeare's and which were Ealer's. For instance:

What man dare, *I* dare!

Approach thou *what* are you laying in the leads for? what a hell of an idea! like the rugged ease her off a little, ease her off! rugged Russian bear, the armed rhinoceros or the *there* she goes! meet her, meet her! didn't you *know* she'd smell the reef if you crowded it like that? Hyrcan tiger; take any shape but that and my firm nerves she'll be in the *woods* the first you know! stop the starboard! come ahead strong on the larboard! back the starboard! . . *Now* then, you're all right; come ahead on the starboard; straighten up and go 'long, never tremble: or be alive again, and dare me to the desert damnation can't you keep away from that greasy water? pull her down! snatch her! snatch her baldheaded! with thy sword; if trembling I inhabit then, lay in the leads!—no, only the starboard one, leave the other alone, protest me the baby of a girl. Hence horrible shadow! eight bells—that watchman's asleep again, I reckon, go down and call Brown yourself, unreal mockery, hence!

He certainly was a good reader, and splendidly thrilling and stormy and tragic, but it was a damage to me, because I have never since been able to read Shakespeare in a calm and sane way. I cannot rid it of his explosive interlardings, they break in everywhere with their irrelevant "What in hell are you up to *now*! pull her down! more! *more*!—there now, steady as you go," and the other disorganizing interruptions that were always leaping from his mouth. When I read Shakespeare now, I can hear them as plainly as I did in that long-departed time—fifty-one years ago. I never regarded Ealer's readings as educational. Indeed they were a detriment to me.

His contributions to the text seldom improved it, but barring that detail he was a good reader, I can say that much for him. He did not use the book, and did not need to; he knew his Shakespeare as well as Euclid ever knew his multiplication table.

Did he have something to say—this Shakespeare-adoring Mississippi pilot—anent Delia Bacon's book? Yes. And he said it; said it all the time, for months—in the morning watch, the middle watch, the dog watch; and probably kept it going in his sleep. He bought the literature of the dispute as fast as it appeared, and we discussed it all through thirteen hundred miles of river four times traversed in every thirty-five days—the time required by that swift boat to achieve two round trips. We discussed, and discussed, and discussed, and disputed and disputed and disputed; at any rate he did, and I got in a word now and then when he slipped a cog and there was a vacancy. He did his arguing with heat, with energy, with violence; and I did mine with the reserve and moderation of a subordinate who does not like to be flung out of a pilot-house that is perched forty feet above the water. He was fiercely loyal to Shakespeare and cordially scornful of Bacon and of all the pretensions of the Baconians. So was I—at first. And at first he was glad that that was my attitude. There were even indications that he admired it; indications dimmed, it is true, by the distance that lay between the lofty boss-pilotical altitude and my lowly one, yet perceptible to me; perceptible, and translatable into a compliment—compliment coming down from above the snow-line and not well thawed in the transit, and not likely to set anything afire, not even a cub-pilot's self-conceit; still a detectable compliment, and precious.

Naturally it flattered me into being more loyal to Shakespeare—if possible—than I was before, and more prejudiced against Bacon—if possible than I was before. And so we discussed and discussed, both on the same side, and were happy. For a while. Only for a while. Only for a very little while, a very, very, very little while. Then the atmosphere began to change; began to cool off.

A brighter person would have seen what the trouble was, earlier than I did, perhaps, but I saw it early enough for all practical purposes. You see, he was of an argumentative disposition. Therefore it took him but a little time to get tired of arguing with a person who agreed with everything he said and consequently never furnished him a provocative to flare up and show what he could do when it came to clear, cold, hard, rose-cut, hundred-faceted, diamond-flashing reasoning. That was his name for it. It has been applied since, with complacency, as many as several times, in the Bacon-Shakespeare scuffle. On the Shakespeare side.

Then the thing happened which has happened to more persons than to me when principle and personal interest found themselves in opposition to each other and a choice had to be made: I let principle go, and went over to the other side. Not the entire way, but far enough to answer the requirements of the case. That is to say, I took this attitude, to wit: I only *believed* Bacon wrote Shakespeare, whereas I *knew* Shakespeare didn't. Ealer was satisfied with that, and the war broke loose. Study, practice, experience in handling my end of the matter presently enabled me to take my new position almost seriously; a little bit later, utterly seriously; a little later still, lovingly, gratefully, devotedly; finally: fiercely, rabidly, uncompromisingly. After that, I was welded to my faith, I was theoretically ready to die for it, and I looked down with compassion not unmixed with scorn, upon everybody else's faith that didn't tally with mine. That faith, imposed upon me by self-interest in that ancient day, remains my faith to-day, and in it I find comfort, solace, peace, and never-failing joy. You see how curiously theological it is. The "rice Christian" of the Orient goes through the very same steps, when he is after rice and the missionary is after *him*; he goes for rice, and remains to worship.

Ealer did a lot of our "reasoning"—not to say substantially all of it. The slaves of his cult have a passion for calling it by that large name. We others do not call our inductions and deductions and reductions by any name at all.

They show for themselves, what they are, and we can with tranquil confidence leave the world to ennoble them with a title of its own choosing.

Now and then when Ealer had to stop to cough, I pulled my induction-talents together and hove the controversial lead myself: always getting eight feet, eight-and-a-half, often nine, sometimes even quarter-less-twain—as *I* believed; but always "no bottom," as *he* said.

I got the best of him only once. I prepared myself. I wrote out a passage from Shakespeare—it may have been the very one I quoted a while ago, I don't remember—and riddled it with his wild steamboatful interlardings. When an unrisky opportunity offered, one lovely summer day, when we had sounded and buoyed a tangled patch of crossings known as Hell's Half Acre, and were aboard again and he had sneaked the Pennsylvania triumphantly through it without once scraping sand, and the *A. T. Lacey* had followed in our wake and got stuck, and he was feeling good, I showed it to him. It amused him. I asked him to fire it off: read it; read it, I diplomatically added, as only he could read dramatic poetry. The compliment touched him where he lived. He did read it; read it with surpassing fire and spirit; read it as it will never be read again; for *he* knew how to put the right music into those thunderous interlardings and make them seem a part of the text, make them sound as if they were bursting from Shakespeare's own soul, each one of them a golden inspiration and not to be left out without damage to the massed and magnificent whole.

I waited a week, to let the incident fade; waited longer; waited until he brought up for reasonings and vituperation my pet position, my pet argument, the one which I was fondest of, the one which I prized far above all others in my ammunition-wagon, to wit: that Shakespeare couldn't have written Shakespeare's works, for the reason that the man who wrote them was limitlessly familiar with the laws, and the law-courts, and law-proceedings, and lawyer-talk, and lawyer-ways—and if Shakespeare was possessed of the infinitely-divided star-dust that constituted this vast wealth, how did he get it, and *where*, and *when*?

"From books."

From books! That was always the idea. I answered as my readings of the champions of my side of the great controversy had taught me to answer: that a man can't handle glibly and easily and comfortably and successfully the *argot* of a trade at which he has not personally served. He will make mistakes; he will not, and cannot, get the trade-phrasings precisely and exactly right; and the moment he departs, by even a shade, from a common trade-form, the reader who has served that trade will know the writer *hasn't*. Ealer would not be convinced; he said a man could learn how to correctly handle the subtleties and mysteries and free-masonries of any trade by careful reading and studying. But when I got him to read again the passage from Shakespeare with the interlardings, he perceived, himself, that books couldn't teach a student a bewildering multitude of pilot-phrases so thoroughly and perfectly that he could talk them off in book and play or conversation and make no mistake that a pilot would not immediately discover. It was a triumph for me. He was silent awhile, and I knew what was happening: he was losing his temper. And I knew he would presently close the session with the same old argument that was always his stay and his support in time of need; the same old argument, the one I couldn't answer—because I dasn't: the argument that I was an ass, and better shut up. He delivered it, and I obeyed.

Oh, dear, how long ago it was—how pathetically long ago! And here am I, old, forsaken, forlorn and alone, arranging to get that argument out of somebody again.

When a man has a passion for Shakespeare, it goes without saying that he keeps company with other standard authors. Ealer always had several high-class books in the pilot-house, and he read the same ones over and over again, and did not care to change to newer and fresher ones. He played well on the flute, and greatly enjoyed hearing himself play. So did I. He had a notion that a flute would keep its health better if you took it apart when it was not standing a watch; and so, when it was not on duty it took its rest, disjointed, on the compass-shelf under the breast-board. When the *Pennsylvania* blew up and became a drifting rack-heap freighted with wounded and dying poor souls (my young brother Henry among them), pilot Brown had the watch below, and was probably asleep and never knew what killed him; but Ealer escaped unhurt. He and his pilot-house were shot up into the air; then they fell, and Ealer sank through the ragged cavern where the hurricane deck and the boiler deck had been, and landed in a nest of ruins on the main deck, on top of one of the unexploded boilers, where he lay prone in a fog of scalding and deadly steam. But not for long. He did not lose his head: long familiarity with danger had taught him to keep it, in any and all emergencies. He held his coat-lappels to his nose with one hand, to keep out the steam, and scrabbled around with the other till he found the joints of his flute, then he is took measures to save himself alive, and was successful. I was not on board. I had been put ashore in New Orleans by Captain Klinefelter. The reason—however, I have told all about it in the book called *Old Times on the Mississippi*, and it isn't important anyway, it is so long ago.

Is Shakespeare Dead?

CHAPTER II

When I was a Sunday-school scholar something more than sixty years ago, I became interested in Satan, and wanted to find out all I could about him. I began to ask questions, but my class-teacher, Mr. Barclay the stone-mason, was reluctant about answering them, it seemed to me. I was anxious to be praised for turning my thoughts to serious subjects when there wasn't another boy in the village who could be hired to do such a thing. I was greatly interested in the incident of Eve and the serpent, and thought Eve's calmness was perfectly noble. I asked Mr. Barclay if he had ever heard of another woman who, being approached by a serpent, would not excuse herself and break for the nearest timber. He did not answer my question, but rebuked me for inquiring into matters above my age and comprehension. I will say for Mr. Barclay that he was willing to tell me the facts of Satan's history, but he stopped there: he wouldn't allow any discussion of them.

In the course of time we exhausted the facts. There were only five or six of them, you could set them all down on a visiting-card. I was disappointed. I had been meditating a biography, and was grieved to find that there were no materials. I said as much, with the tears running down. Mr. Barclay's sympathy and compassion were aroused, for he was a most kind and gentle-spirited man, and he patted me on the head and cheered me up by saying there was a whole vast ocean of materials! I can still feel the happy thrill which these blessed words shot through me.

Then he began to bail out that ocean's riches for my encouragement and joy. Like this: it was "conjectured"—though not established—that Satan was originally an angel in heaven; that he fell; that he rebelled, and brought on a war; that he was defeated, and banished to perdition. Also, "we have reason to believe" that later he did so-and-so; that "we are warranted in supposing" that at a subsequent time he travelled extensively, seeking whom he might devour; that a couple of centuries afterward, "as tradition instructs us," he took up the cruel trade of tempting people to their ruin, with vast and fearful results; that by-and-by, "as the probabilities seem to indicate," he may have done certain things, he might have done certain other things, he must have done still other things.

And so on and so on. We set down the five known facts by themselves, on a piece of paper, and numbered it "page 1"; then on fifteen hundred other pieces of paper we set down the "conjectures," and "suppositions," and "maybes," and "perhapses," and "doubtlesses," and "rumors," and "guesses," and "probabilities," and "likelihoods," and "we are permitted to thinks," and "we are warranted in believings," and "might have beens," and "could have beens," and "must have beens," and "unquestionablys," and "without a shadow of doubts"—and behold!

Materials? Why, we had enough to build a biography of Shakespeare!

Yet he made me put away my pen; he would not let me write the history of Satan. Why? Because, as he said, he had suspicions; suspicions that my attitude in this matter was not reverent; and that a person must be reverent when writing about the sacred characters. He said any one who spoke flippantly of Satan would be frowned upon by the religious world and also be brought to account.

I assured him, in earnest and sincere words, that he had wholly misconceived my attitude; that I had the highest respect for Satan, and that my reverence for him equalled, and possibly even exceeded, that of any member of any church. I said it wounded me deeply to perceive by his words that he thought I would make fun of Satan, and deride him, laugh at him, scoff at him: whereas in truth I had never thought of such a thing, but had only a warm desire to make fun of those others and laugh at *them*. "What others?" "Why, the Supposers, the Perhapsers, the Might-Have-Beeners, the Could-Have-Beeners, the Must-Have-Beeners, the Without-a-Shadow-of-Doubters, the We-are-Warranted-in-Believingers, and all that funny crop of solemn architects who have taken a good solid foundation of five indisputable and unimportant facts and built upon it a Conjectural Satan thirty miles high."

What did Mr. Barclay do then? Was he disarmed? Was he silenced? No. He was shocked. He was so shocked that he visibly shuddered. He said the Satanic Traditioners and Perhapsers and Conjecturers were *themselves* sacred! As sacred as their work. So sacred that whoso ventured to mock them or make fun of their work, could not afterward enter any respectable house, even by the back door.

How true were his words, and how wise! How fortunate it would have been for me if I had heeded them. But I was young, I was but seven years of age, and vain, foolish, and anxious to attract attention. I wrote the biography, and have never been in a respectable house since.

Is Shakespeare Dead?

CHAPTER III

How curious and interesting is the parallel—as far as poverty of biographical details is concerned—between Satan and Shakespeare. It is wonderful, it is unique, it stands quite alone, there is nothing resembling it in history, nothing resembling it in romance, nothing approaching it even in tradition. How sublime is their position, and how over-topping, how sky-reaching, how supreme—the two Great Unknowns, the two Illustrious Conjecturabilities! They are the best-known unknown persons that have ever drawn breath upon the planet.

For the instruction of the ignorant I will make a list, now, of those details of Shakespeare's history which are *facts*—verified facts, established facts, undisputed facts.

FACTS

He was born on the 23d of April, 1564.

Of good farmer-class parents who could not read, could not write, could not sign their names.

At Stratford, a small back settlement which in that day was shabby and unclean, and densely illiterate. Of the nineteen important men charged with the government of the town, thirteen had to "make their mark" in attesting important documents, because they could not write their names.

Of the first eighteen years of his life *nothing* is known. They are a blank.

On the 27th of November (1582) William Shakespeare took out a license to marry Anne Whateley.

Next day William Shakespeare took out a license to marry Anne Hathaway. She was eight years his senior.

William Shakespeare married Anne Hathaway. In a hurry. By grace of a reluctantly-granted dispensation there was but one publication of the banns.

Within six months the first child was born.

About two (blank) years followed, during which period *nothing at all happened to Shakespeare*, so far as anybody knows.

Then came twins—1585. February.

Two blank years follow.

Then—1587—he makes a ten-year visit to London, leaving the family behind.

Five blank years follow. During this period *nothing happened to him*, as far as anybody actually knows.

Then—1592—there is mention of him as an actor.

Next year—1593—his name appears in the official list of players.

Next year—1594—he played before the queen. A detail of no consequence: other obscurities did it every year of the forty-five of her reign. And remained obscure.

Three pretty full years follow. Full of play-acting. Then

In 1597 he bought New Place, Stratford.

Thirteen or fourteen busy years follow; years in which he accumulated money, and also reputation as actor and manager.

Meantime his name, liberally and variously spelt, had become associated with a number of great plays and poems, as (ostensibly) author of the same.

Some of these, in these years and later, were pirated, but he made no protest. Then—1610-11—he returned to Stratford and settled down for good and all, and busied himself in lending money, trading in tithes, trading in land and houses; shirking a debt of forty-one shillings, borrowed by his wife during his long desertion of his family; suing debtors for shillings and coppers; being sued himself for shillings and coppers; and acting as confederate to a neighbor who tried to rob the town of its rights in a certain common, and did not succeed.

He lived five or six years—till 1616—in the joy of these elevated pursuits. Then he made a will, and signed each of its three pages with his name.

A thoroughgoing business man's will. It named in minute detail every item of property he owned in the world—houses, lands, sword, silver-gilt bowl, and so on—all the way down to his "second-best bed" and its furniture.

It carefully and calculatingly distributed his riches among the members of his family, overlooking no individual of it. Not even his wife: the wife he had been enabled to marry in a hurry by urgent grace of a special dispensation before he was nineteen; the wife whom he had left husbandless so many years; the wife who had had to borrow forty-one shillings in her need, and which the lender was never able to collect of the prosperous husband, but died at last with the money still lacking. No, even this wife was remembered in Shakespeare's will.

He left her that "second-best bed."

And *not another thing*; not even a penny to bless her lucky widowhood with.

It was eminently and conspicuously a business man's will, not a poet's.

It mentioned not a single book.

Books were much more precious than swords and silver-gilt bowls and second-best beds in those days, and when a departing person owned one he gave it a high place in his will.

The will mentioned not a play, not a poem, not an unfinished literary work, not a scrap of manuscript of any kind.

Many poets have died poor, but this is the only one in history that has died *this* poor; the others all left literary remains behind. Also a book. Maybe two.

Is Shakespeare Dead?

If Shakespeare had owned a dog—but we need not go into that: we know he would have mentioned it in his will. If a good dog, Susanna would have got it; if an inferior one his wife would have got a dower interest in it. I wish he had had a dog, just so we could see how painstakingly he would have divided that dog among the family, in his careful business way.

He signed the will in three places.

In earlier years he signed two other official documents.

These five signatures still exist.

There are no other specimens of his penmanship in existence. Not a line.

Was he prejudiced against the art? His granddaughter, whom he loved, was eight years old when he died, yet she had had no teaching, he left no provision for her education although he was rich, and in her mature womanhood she couldn't write and couldn't tell her husband's manuscript from anybody else's—she thought it was Shakespeare's.

When Shakespeare died in Stratford *it was not an event*. It made no more stir in England than the death of any other forgotten theatre-actor would have made. Nobody came down from London; there were no lamenting poems, no eulogies, no national tears—there was merely silence, and nothing more. A striking contrast with what happened when Ben Jonson, and Francis Bacon, and Spenser, and Raleigh and the other distinguished literary folk of Shakespeare's time passed from life! No praiseful voice was lifted for the lost Bard of Avon; even Ben Jonson waited seven years before he lifted his.

So far as anybody actually knows and can prove, Shakespeare of Stratford-on-Avon never wrote a play in his life.

So far as anybody knows and can prove, he never wrote a letter to anybody in his life.

So far as any one knows, he received only one letter during his life.

So far as any one *knows and can prove*, Shakespeare of Stratford wrote only one poem during his life. This one is authentic. He did write that one—a fact which stands undisputed; he wrote the whole of it; he wrote the whole of it out of his own head. He commanded that this work of art be engraved upon his tomb, and he was obeyed. There it abides to this day. This is it:

> *Good friend for Iesus sake forbeare*
> *To digg the dust encloased heare:*
> *Blest be ye man yt spares thes stones*
> *And curst be he yt moves my bones.*

In the list as above set down, will be found *every positively known* fact of Shakespeare's life, lean and meagre as the invoice is. Beyond these details we know *not a thing* about him. All the rest of his vast history, as furnished by the biographers, is built up, course upon course, of guesses, inferences, theories, conjectures—an Eiffel Tower of artificialities rising sky-high from a very flat and very thin foundation of inconsequential facts.

Is Shakespeare Dead?

CHAPTER IV

CONJECTURES

The historians "suppose" that Shakespeare attended the Free School in Stratford from the time he was seven years old till he was thirteen. There is no *evidence* in existence that he ever went to school at all.

The historians "infer" that he got his Latin in that school—the school which they "suppose" he attended.

They "suppose" his father's declining fortunes made it necessary for him to leave the school they supposed he attended, and get to work and help support his parents and their ten children. But there is no evidence that he ever entered or retired from the school they suppose he attended.

They "suppose" he assisted his father in the butchering business; and that, being only a boy, he didn't have to do full-grown butchering, but only slaughtered calves. Also, that whenever he killed a calf he made a high-flown speech over it. This supposition rests upon the testimony of a man who wasn't there at the time; a man who got it from a man who could have been there, but did not say whether he was or not; and neither of them thought to mention it for decades, and decades, and decades, and two more decades after Shakespeare's death (until old age and mental decay had refreshed and vivified their memories). They hadn't two facts in stock about the long-dead distinguished citizen, but only just the one: he slaughtered calves and broke into oratory while he was at it. Curious. They had only one fact, yet the distinguished citizen had spent twenty-six years in that little town—just half his lifetime. However, rightly viewed, it was the most important fact, indeed almost the only important fact, of Shakespeare's life in Stratford. Rightly viewed. For experience is an author's most valuable asset; experience is the thing that puts the muscle and the breath and the warm blood into the book he writes. Rightly viewed, calf-butchering accounts for *Titus Andronicus*, the only play—ain't it?—that the Stratford Shakespeare ever wrote; and yet it is the only one everybody tries to chouse him out of, the Baconians included.

The historians find themselves "justified in believing" that the young Shakespeare poached upon Sir Thomas Lucy's deer preserves and got haled before that magistrate for it. But there is no shred of respectworthy evidence that anything of the kind happened.

The historians, having argued the thing that *might* have happened into the thing that *did* happen, found no trouble in turning Sir Thomas Lucy into Mr. Justice Shallow. They have long ago convinced the world—on surmise and without trustworthy evidence—that Shallow *is* Sir Thomas.

The next addition to the young Shakespeare's Stratford history comes easy. The historian builds it out of the surmised deer-stealing, and the surmised trial before the magistrate, and the surmised vengeance-prompted satire upon the magistrate in the play: result, the young Shakespeare was a wild, wild, wild, oh *such* a wild young scamp, and that gratuitous slander is established for all time! It is the very way Professor Osborn and I built the colossal skeleton brontosaur that stands fifty-seven feet long and sixteen feet high in the Natural History Museum, the awe and admiration of all the world, the stateliest skeleton that exists on the planet. We had nine bones, and we built the rest of him out of plaster of paris. We ran short of plaster of paris, or we'd have built a brontosaur that could sit down beside the Stratford Shakespeare and none but an expert could tell which was biggest or contained the most plaster.

Shakespeare pronounced *Venus and Adonis* "the first heir of his invention," apparently implying that it was his first effort at literary composition. He should not have said it. It has been an embarrassment to his historians these many, many years. They have to make him write that graceful and polished and flawless and beautiful poem before he escaped from Stratford and his family—1586 or '87—age, twenty-two, or along there; because within the next five years he wrote five great plays, and could not have found time to write another line.

It is sorely embarrassing. If he began to slaughter calves, and poach deer, and rollick around, and learn English, at the earliest likely moment—say at thirteen, when he was supposably wrenched from that school where he was supposably storing up Latin for future literary use—he had his youthful hands full, and much more than full. He must have had to put aside his Warwickshire dialect, which wouldn't be understood in London, and study English very hard. Very hard indeed; incredibly hard, almost, if the result of that labor was to be the smooth and rounded and flexible and letter-perfect English of the *Venus and Adonis* in the space of ten years; and at the same time learn great and fine and unsurpassable literary form.

However, it is "conjectured" that he accomplished all this and more, much more: learned law and its intricacies; and the complex procedure of the law courts; and all about soldiering, and sailoring, and the manners and customs and ways of royal courts and aristocratic society; and likewise accumulated in his one head every kind of knowledge the learned then possessed, and every kind of humble knowledge possessed by the lowly and the ignorant; and added thereto a wider and more intimate knowledge of the world's great literatures, ancient and modern, than was possessed by any other man of his time—for he was going to make brilliant and easy and admiration-compelling use of these splendid treasures the moment he got to London. And according to the surmisers, that is what he did. Yes, although there was no one in Stratford able to teach him these things, and no library in the little village to dig them out of. His father could not read, and even the surmisers surmise that he did not keep a library.

It is surmised by the biographers that the young Shakespeare got his vast knowledge of the law and his familiar and accurate acquaintance with the manners and customs and shop-talk of lawyers through being for a time the *clerk of a Stratford court*; just as a bright lad like me, reared in a village on the banks of the Mississippi, might become perfect in knowledge of the Behring Strait whale-fishery and the shop-talk of the veteran exercisers of that adventure-bristling trade through catching catfish with a "trot-line" Sundays. But the surmise is damaged by the fact that there is no evidence—and not even tradition—that the young Shakespeare was ever clerk of a law court.

It is further surmised that the young Shakespeare accumulated his law-treasures in the first years of his sojourn in London, through "amusing himself" by learning book-law in his garret and by picking up lawyer-talk and the rest of it through loitering about the law-courts and listening. But it is only surmise; there is no *evidence* that he ever did either of those things. They are merely a couple of chunks of plaster of paris.

There is a legend that he got his bread and butter by holding horses in front of the London theatres, mornings and afternoons. Maybe he did. If he did, it seriously shortened his law-study hours and his recreation-time in the courts. In those very days he was writing great plays, and needed all the time he could get. The horse-holding legend ought to be strangled; it too formidably increases the historian's difficulty in accounting for the young Shakespeare's erudition—an erudition which he was acquiring, hunk by hunk and chunk by chunk every day in those strenuous times, and emptying each day's catch into next day's imperishable drama.

He had to acquire a knowledge of war at the same time; and a knowledge of soldier-people and sailor-people and their ways and talk; also a knowledge of some foreign lands and their languages: for he was daily emptying fluent streams of these various knowledges, too, into his dramas. How did he acquire these rich assets?

In the usual way: by surmise. It is *surmised* that he travelled in Italy and Germany and around, and qualified himself to put their scenic and social aspects upon paper; that he perfected himself in French, Italian and Spanish on the road; that he went in Leicester's expedition to the Low Countries, as soldier or sutler or something, for several months or years—or whatever length of time a surmiser needs in his business—and thus became familiar with soldiership and soldier-ways and soldier-talk, and generalship and general-ways and general-talk, and seamanship and sailor-ways and sailor-talk.

Maybe he did all these things, but I would like to know who held the horses in the meantime; and who studied the books in the garret; and who frollicked in the law-courts for recreation. Also, who did the call-boying and the play-acting.

For he became a call-boy; and as early as '93 he became a "vagabond"—the law's ungentle term for an unlisted actor; and in '94 a "regular" and properly and officially listed member of that (in those days) lightly-valued and not much respected profession.

Right soon thereafter he became a stockholder in two theatres, and manager of them. Thenceforward he was a busy and flourishing business man, and was raking in money with both hands for twenty years. Then in a noble frenzy of poetic inspiration he wrote his one poem—his only poem, his darling—and laid him down and died:

> *Good friend for Iesus sake forbeare*
> *To digg the dust encloased heare:*
> *Blest be ye man yt spares thes stones*
> *And curst be he yt moves my bones.*

He was probably dead when he wrote it. Still, this is only conjecture. We have only circumstantial evidence. Internal evidence.

Shall I set down the rest of the Conjectures which constitute the giant Biography of William Shakespeare? It would strain the Unabridged Dictionary to hold them. He is a Brontosaur: nine bones and six hundred barrels of plaster of paris.

Is Shakespeare Dead?

CHAPTER V

"We May Assume"

In the Assuming trade three separate and independent cults are transacting business. Two of these cults are known as the Shakespearites and the Baconians, and I am the other one—the Brontosaurian.

The Shakespearite knows that Shakespeare wrote Shakespeare's Works; the Baconian knows that Francis Bacon wrote them; the Brontosaurian doesn't really know which of them did it, but is quite composedly and contentedly sure that Shakespeare *didn't*, and strongly suspects that Bacon *did*. We all have to do a good deal of assuming, but I am fairly certain that in every case I can call to mind the Baconian assumers have come out ahead of the Shakespearites. Both parties handle the same materials, but the Baconians seem to me to get much more reasonable and rational and persuasive results out of them than is the case with the Shakespearites. The Shakespearite conducts his assuming upon a definite principle, an unchanging and immutable law—which is: 2 and 8 and 7 and 14, added together, make 165. I believe this to be an error. No matter, you cannot get a habit-sodden Shakespearite to cipher-up his materials upon any other basis. With the Baconian it is different. If you place before him the above figures and set him to adding them up, he will never in any case get more than 45 out of them, and in nine cases out of ten he will get just the proper 31.

Let me try to illustrate the two systems in a simple and homely way calculated to bring the idea within the grasp of the ignorant and unintelligent. We will suppose a case: take a lap-bred, house-fed, uneducated, inexperienced kitten; take a rugged old Tom that's scarred from stem to rudder-post with the memorials of strenuous experience, and is so cultured, so educated, so limitlessly erudite that one may say of him "all cat-knowledge is his province"; also, take a mouse. Lock the three up in a holeless, crackless, exitless prison-cell. Wait half an hour, then open the cell, introduce a Shakespearite and a Baconian, and let them cipher and assume. The mouse is missing: the question to be decided is, where is it? You can guess both verdicts beforehand. One verdict will say the kitten contains the mouse; the other will as certainly say the mouse is in the tomcat.

The Shakespearite will Reason like this—(that is not my word, it is his). He will say the kitten *may have been* attending school when nobody was noticing; therefore *we are warranted in assuming* that it did so; also, it *could have been* training in a court-clerk's office when no one was noticing; since that could have happened, *we are justified in assuming* that it did happen; it *could have studied catology in a garret* when no one was noticing—therefore it *did*; it *could have* attended cat-assizes on the shed-roof nights, for recreation, when no one was noticing, and harvested a knowledge of cat court-forms and cat lawyer-talk in that way: it *could* have done it, therefore without a doubt it did; it could have gone soldiering with a war-tribe when no one was noticing, and learned soldier-wiles and soldier-ways, and what to do with a mouse when opportunity offers; the plain inference, therefore is, that that is what it *did*. Since all these manifold things *could* have occurred, we have *every right to believe* they did occur. These patiently and painstakingly accumulated vast acquirements and competences needed but one thing more—opportunity—to convert themselves into triumphant action. The opportunity came, we have the result; *beyond shadow of question* the mouse is in the kitten.

It is proper to remark that when we of the three cults plant a *"We think we may assume,"* we expect it, under careful watering and fertilizing and tending, to grow up into a strong and hardy and weather-defying *"there isn't a shadow of a doubt"* at last—and it usually happens.

We know what the Baconian's verdict would be: "There is not a rag of evidence that the kitten has had any training, any education, any experience qualifying it for the present occasion, or is indeed equipped for any achievement above lifting such unclaimed milk as comes its way; but there is abundant evidence—unassailable proof, in fact—that the other animal is equipped, to the last detail, with every qualification necessary for the event. Without shadow of doubt the tomcat contains the mouse."

Is Shakespeare Dead?

CHAPTER VI

When Shakespeare died, in 1616, great literary productions attributed to him as author had been before the London world and in high favor for twenty-four years. Yet his death was not an event. It made no stir, it attracted no attention. Apparently his eminent literary contemporaries did not realize that a celebrated poet had passed from their midst. Perhaps they knew a play-actor of minor rank had disappeared, but did not regard him as the author of his Works. "We are justified in assuming" this.

His death was not even an event in the little town of Stratford. Does this mean that in Stratford he was not regarded as a celebrity of *any* kind?

"We are privileged to assume"—no, we are indeed *obliged* to assume—that such was the case. He had spent the first twenty-two or twenty-three years of his life there, and of course knew everybody and was known by everybody of that day in the town, including the dogs and the cats and the horses. He had spent the last five or six years of his life there, diligently trading in every big and little thing that had money in it; so we are compelled to assume that many of the folk there in those said latter days knew him personally, and the rest by sight and hearsay. But not as a *celebrity*? Apparently not. For everybody soon forgot to remember any contact with him or any incident connected with him. The dozens of townspeople, still alive, who had known of him or known about him in the first twenty-three years of his life were in the same unremembering condition: if they knew of any incident connected with that period of his life they didn't tell about it. Would they if they had been asked? It is most likely. Were they asked? It is pretty apparent that they were not. Why weren't they? It is a very plausible guess that nobody there or elsewhere was interested to know.

For seven years after Shakespeare's death nobody seems to have been interested in him. Then the quarto was published, and Ben Jonson awoke out of his long indifference and sang a song of praise and put it in the front of the book. Then silence fell *again*.

For sixty years. Then inquiries into Shakespeare's Stratford life began to be made, of Stratfordians. Of Stratfordians who had known Shakespeare or had seen him? No. Then of Stratfordians who had seen people who had known or seen people who had seen Shakespeare? No. Apparently the inquiries were only made of Stratfordians who were not Stratfordians of Shakespeare's day, but later comers; and what they had learned had come to them from persons who had not seen Shakespeare; and what they had learned was not claimed as *fact*, but only as legend—dim and fading and indefinite legend; legend of the calf-slaughtering rank, and not worth remembering either as history or fiction.

Has it ever happened before—or since—that a celebrated person who had spent exactly half of a fairly long life in the village where he was born and reared, was able to slip out of this world and leave that village voiceless and gossipless behind him—utterly voiceless, utterly gossipless? And permanently so? I don't believe it has happened in any case except Shakespeare's. And couldn't and wouldn't have happened in his case if he had been regarded as a celebrity at the time of his death.

When I examine my own case—but let us do that, and see if it will not be recognizable as exhibiting a condition of things quite likely to result, most likely to result, indeed substantially *sure* to result in the case of a celebrated person, a benefactor of the human race. Like me.

My parents brought me to the village of Hannibal, Missouri, on the banks of the Mississippi, when I was two and a half years old. I entered school at five years of age, and drifted from one school to another in the village during nine and a half years. Then my father died, leaving his family in exceedingly straitened circumstances; wherefore my book-education came to a standstill forever, and I became a printer's apprentice, on board and clothes, and when the clothes failed I got a hymn-book in place of them. This for summer wear, probably. I lived in Hannibal fifteen and a half years, altogether, then ran away, according to the custom of persons who are intending to become celebrated. I never lived there afterward. Four years later I became a "cub" on a Mississippi steamboat in the St. Louis and New Orleans trade, and after a year and a half of hard study and hard work the U. S. inspectors rigorously examined me through a couple of long sittings and decided that I knew every inch of the Mississippi—thirteen hundred miles—in the dark and in the day—as well as a baby knows the way to its mother's paps day or night. So they licensed me as a pilot—knighted me, so to speak—and I rose up clothed with authority, a responsible servant of the United States government.

Now then. Shakespeare died young—he was only fifty-two. He had lived in his native village twenty-six years, or about that. He died celebrated (if you believe everything you read in the books). Yet when he died nobody there or elsewhere took any notice of it; and for sixty years afterward no townsman remembered to say anything about him or about his life in Stratford. When the inquirer came at last he got but one fact—no, *legend*—and got that one at second hand, from a person who had only heard it as a rumor, and didn't claim copyright in it as a production of his own. He couldn't, very well, for its date antedated his own birth-date. But necessarily a number of persons were still alive in Stratford who, in the days of their youth, had seen Shakespeare nearly every day in the last five years of his life, and they would have been able to tell that inquirer some first-hand things about him if he had in those last days been a celebrity and therefore a person of interest to the villagers. Why did not the inquirer hunt them up and interview them? Wasn't it worth while? Wasn't the matter of sufficient consequence? Had the inquirer an engagement to see a dog-fight and couldn't spare the time?

It all seems to mean that he never had any literary celebrity, there or elsewhere, and no considerable repute as actor and manager.

Now then, I am away along in life—my seventy-third year being already well behind me—yet *sixteen* of my Hannibal schoolmates are still alive to-day, and can tell—and do tell—inquirers dozens and dozens of incidents of their young lives and mine together; things that happened to us in the morning of life, in the blossom of our youth, in the good days, the dear days, "the days when we went gipsying, a long time ago." Most of them creditable to me, too. One child to whom I paid court when she was five years old and I eight still lives in Hannibal, and she visited me last summer, traversing the necessary ten or twelve hundred miles of railroad without damage to her patience or to her old-young vigor. Another little lassie to whom I paid attention in Hannibal when she was nine years old and I the same, is still alive—in London—and hale and hearty, just as I am. And on the few surviving steamboats—those lingering ghosts and remembrancers of great fleets that plied the big river in the beginning of my water-career— which is exactly as long ago as the whole invoice of the life-years of Shakespeare number—there are still findable two or three river-pilots who saw me do creditable things in those ancient days; and several white-headed engineers; and several roustabouts and mates; and several deck-hands who used to heave the lead for me and send up on the still night air the "six— feet—*scant*!" that made me shudder, and the "*M-a-r-k—twain*!" that took the shudder away, and presently the darling "By the d-e-e-p—four!" that lifted me to heaven for joy.[1] They know about me, and can tell. And so do printers, from St. Louis to New York; and so do newspaper reporters, from Nevada to San Francisco. And so do the police. If Shakespeare had really been celebrated, like me, Stratford could have told things about him; and if my experience goes for anything, they'd have done it.

---

[1] Four fathoms—twenty-four feet.

Mark Twain

CHAPTER VII

If I had under my superintendence a controversy appointed to decide whether Shakespeare wrote Shakespeare or not, I believe I would place before the debaters only the one question, *Was Shakespeare ever a practicing lawyer?* and leave everything else out.

It is maintained that the man who wrote the plays was not merely myriad-minded, but also myriad-accomplished: that he not only knew some thousands of things about human life in all its shades and grades, and about the hundred arts and trades and crafts and professions which men busy themselves in, but that he could *talk* about the men and their grades and trades accurately, making no mistakes. Maybe it is so, but have the experts spoken, or is it only Tom, Dick, and Harry? Does the exhibit stand upon wide, and loose, and eloquent generalizing—which is not evidence, and not proof—or upon details, particulars, statistics, illustrations, demonstrations?

Experts of unchallengeable authority have testified definitely as to only one of Shakespeare's multifarious craft-equipments, so far as my recollections of Shakespeare-Bacon talk abide with me—his law-equipment. I do not remember that Wellington or Napoleon ever examined Shakespeare's battles and sieges and strategies, and then decided and established for good and all, that they were militarily flawless; I do not remember that any Nelson, or Drake or Cook ever examined his seamanship and said it showed profound and accurate familiarity with that art; I don't remember that any king or prince or duke has ever testified that Shakespeare was letter-perfect in his handling of royal court-manners and the talk and manners of aristocracies; I don't remember that any illustrious Latinist or Grecian or Frenchman or Spaniard or Italian has proclaimed him a past-master in those languages; I don't remember—well, I don't remember that there is *testimony*—great testimony—imposing testimony—unanswerable and unattackable testimony as to any of Shakespeare's hundred specialties, except one—the law.

Other things change, with time, and the student cannot trace back with certainty the changes that various trades and their processes and technicalities have undergone in the long stretch of a century or two and find out what their processes and technicalities were in those early days, but with the law it is different: it is mile-stoned and documented all the way back, and the master of that wonderful trade, that complex and intricate trade, that awe-compelling trade, has competent ways of knowing whether Shakespeare-law is good law or not; and whether his law-court procedure is correct or not, and whether his legal shop-talk is the shop-talk of a veteran practitioner or only a machine-made counterfeit of it gathered from books and from occasional loiterings in Westminster.

Richard H. Dana served two years before the mast, and had every experience that falls to the lot of the sailor before the mast of our day. His sailor-talk flows from his pen with the sure touch and the ease and confidence of a person who has *lived* what he is talking about, not gathered it from books and random listenings. Hear him:

Having hove short, cast off the gaskets, and made the bunt of each sail fast by the jigger, with a man on each yard, at the word the whole canvas of the ship was loosed, and with the greatest rapidity possible everything was sheeted home and hoisted up, the anchor tripped and cat-headed, and the ship under headway.

Again:

The royal yards were all crossed at once, and royals and sky-sails set, and, as we had the wind free, the booms were run out, and all were aloft, active as cats, laying out on the yards and booms, reeving the studding-sail gear; and sail after sail the captain piled upon her, until she was covered with canvas, her sails looking like a great white cloud resting upon a black speck.

Once more. A race in the Pacific:

Our antagonist was in her best trim. Being clear of the point, the breeze became stiff, and the royal-masts bent under our sails, but we would not take them in until we saw three boys spring into the rigging of the *California*;

then they were all furled at once, but with orders to our boys to stay aloft at the top-gallant mast-heads and loose them again at the word. It was my duty to furl the fore-royal; and while standing by to loose it again, I had a fine view of the scene. From where I stood, the two vessels seemed nothing but spars and sails, while their narrow decks, far below, slanting over by the force of the wind aloft, appeared hardly capable of supporting the great fabrics raised upon them. The *California* was to windward of us, and had every advantage; yet, while the breeze was stiff we held our own. As soon as it began to slacken she ranged a little ahead, and the order was given to loose the royals. In an instant the gaskets were off and the bunt dropped. "Sheet home the fore-royal!"—"Weather sheet's home!"—"Lee sheet's home!"—"Hoist away, sir!" is bawled from aloft. "Overhaul your clewlines!" shouts the mate. "Aye-aye, sir, all clear!"—"Taut leech! belay! Well the lee brace; haul taut to windward!" and the royals are set.

What would the captain of any sailing-vessel of our time say to that? He would say, "The man that wrote that didn't learn his trade out of a book, he has *been* there!" But would this same captain be competent to sit in judgment upon Shakespeare's seamanship—considering the changes in ships and ship-talk that have necessarily taken place, unrecorded, unremembered, and lost to history in the last three hundred years? It is my conviction that Shakespeare's sailor-talk would be Choctaw to him. For instance—from *The Tempest*:

Master. Boatswain!

Boatswain. Here, master; what cheer?

Master. Good, speak to the mariners: fall to't, yarely, or we run ourselves to ground; bestir, bestir!

(Enter mariners.)

Boatswain. Heigh, my hearts! cheerly, cheerly, my hearts! yare, yare! Take in the topsail. Tend to the master's whistle . . . Down with the topmast! yare! lower, lower! Bring her to try wi' the main course . . . Lay her a-hold, a-hold! Set her two courses. Off to sea again; lay her off.

That will do, for the present; let us yare a little, now, for a change.

If a man should write a book and in it make one of his characters say, "Here, devil, empty the quoins into the standing galley and the imposing stone into the hell-box; assemble the comps around the frisket and let them jeff for takes and be quick about it," I should recognize a mistake or two in the phrasing, and would know that the writer was only a printer theoretically, not practically.

I have been a quartz miner in the silver regions—a pretty hard life; I know all the palaver of that business: I know all about discovery claims and the subordinate claims; I know all about lodes, ledges, outcroppings, dips, spurs, angles, shafts, drifts, inclines, levels, tunnels, air-shafts, "horses," clay casings, granite casings; quartz mills and their batteries; arastras, and how to charge them with quicksilver and sulphate of copper; and how to clean them up, and how to reduce the resulting amalgam in the retorts, and how to cast the bullion into pigs; and finally I know how to screen tailings, and also how to hunt for something less robust to do, and find it. I know the *argot* of the quartz-mining and milling industry familiarly; and so whenever Bret Harte introduces that industry into a story, the first time one of his miners opens his mouth I recognize from his phrasing that Harte got the phrasing by listening—like Shakespeare—I mean the Stratford one—not by experience. No one can talk the quartz dialect correctly without learning it with pick and shovel and drill and fuse.

I have been a surface-miner—gold—and I know all its mysteries, and the dialect that belongs with them; and whenever Harte introduces that industry into a story I know by the phrasing of his characters that neither he nor they have ever served that trade.

I have been a "pocket" miner—a sort of gold mining not findable in any but one little spot in the world, so far as I know. I know how, with horn and water, to find the trail of a pocket and trace it step by step and stage by stage up the mountain to its source, and find the compact little nest of yellow metal reposing in its secret home under the ground. I know the language of that trade, that capricious trade, that fascinating buried-treasure trade, and can catch any writer who tries to use it without having learned it by the sweat of his brow and the labor of his hands.

I know several other trades and the *argot* that goes with them; and whenever a person tries to talk the talk peculiar to any of them without having learned it at its source I can trap him always before he gets far on his road.

And so, as I have already remarked, if I were required to superintend a Bacon-Shakespeare controversy, I would narrow the matter down to a single question—the only one, so far as the previous controversies have informed me, concerning which illustrious experts of unimpeachable competency have testified: *Was the author of Shakespeare's Works a lawyer?*—a lawyer deeply read and of limitless experience? I would put aside the guesses, and surmises, and perhapses, and might-have-beens, and could-have beens, and must-have-beens, and we-are justified-in-presumings, and the rest of those vague spectres and shadows and indefinitenesses, and stand or fall, win or lose, by the verdict rendered by the jury upon that single question. If the verdict was Yes, I should feel quite convinced that the Stratford Shakespeare, the actor, manager, and trader who died so obscure, so forgotten, so destitute of even village consequence that sixty years afterward no fellow-citizen and friend of his later days remembered to tell anything about him, did not write the Works.

Chapter XIII of *The Shakespeare Problem Restated* bears the heading "Shakespeare as a Lawyer," and comprises some fifty pages of expert testimony, with comments thereon, and I will copy the first nine, as being sufficient all by themselves, as it seems to me, to settle the question which I have conceived to be the master-key to the Shakespeare-Bacon puzzle.

Is Shakespeare Dead?

CHAPTER VIII

Shakespeare as a Lawyer[2]

The Plays and Poems of Shakespeare supply ample evidence that their author not only had a very extensive and accurate knowledge of law, but that he was well acquainted with the manners and customs of members of the Inns of Court and with legal life generally.

"While novelists and dramatists are constantly making mistakes as to the laws of marriage, of wills, and inheritance, to Shakespeare's law, lavishly as he expounds it, there can neither be demurrer, nor bill of exceptions, nor writ of error." Such was the testimony borne by one of the most distinguished lawyers of the nineteenth century who was raised to the high office of Lord Chief Justice in 1850, and subsequently became Lord Chancellor. Its weight will, doubtless, be more appreciated by lawyers than by laymen, for only lawyers know how impossible it is for those who have not served an apprenticeship to the law to avoid displaying their ignorance if they venture to employ legal terms and to discuss legal doctrines. "There is nothing so dangerous," wrote Lord Campbell, "as for one not of the craft to tamper with our freemasonry." A layman is certain to betray himself by using some expression which a lawyer would never employ. Mr. Sidney Lee himself supplies us with an example of this. He writes (p. 164): "On February 15, 1609, Shakespeare . . . obtained judgment from a jury against Addenbroke for the payment of No. 6, and No. 1. 5*s*. 0*d*. costs." Now a

---

[2] From chapter XIII of "The Shakespeare Problem Restated."

lawyer would never have spoken of obtaining "judgment from a jury," for it is the function of a jury not to deliver judgment (which is the prerogative of the court), but to find a verdict on the facts. The error is, indeed, a venial one, but it is just one of those little things which at once enable a lawyer to know if the writer is a layman or "one of the craft."

But when a layman ventures to plunge deeply into legal subjects, he is naturally apt to make an exhibition of his incompetence. "Let a non-professional man, however acute," writes Lord Campbell again, "presume to talk law, or to draw illustrations from legal science in discussing other subjects, and he will speedily fall into laughable absurdity."

And what does the same high authority say about Shakespeare? He had "a deep technical knowledge of the law," and an easy familiarity with "some of the most abstruse proceedings in English jurisprudence." And again: "Whenever he indulges this propensity he uniformly lays down good law." Of *Henry IV.*, Part 2, he says: "If Lord Eldon could be supposed to have written the play, I do not see how he could be chargeable with having forgotten any of his law while writing it." Charles and Mary Cowden Clarke speak of "the marvelous intimacy which he displays with legal terms, his frequent adoption of them in illustration, and his curiously technical knowledge of their form and force." Malone, himself a lawyer, wrote: "His knowledge of legal terms is not merely such as might be acquired by the casual observation of even his all-comprehending mind; it has the appearance of technical skill." Another lawyer and well-known Shakespearean, Richard Grant White, says: "No dramatist of the time, not even Beaumont, who was the younger son of a judge of the Common Pleas, and who after studying in the Inns of Court abandoned law for the drama, used legal phrases with Shakespeare's readiness and exactness. And the significance of this fact is heightened by another, that it is only to the language of the law that he exhibits this inclination. The phrases peculiar to other occupations serve him on rare occasions by way of description, comparison or illustration, generally when something in the scene suggests them, but legal phrases flow from his pen as part of his vocabulary, and parcel of his thought. Take the word 'purchase' for instance, which, in ordinary use, means to acquire by giving value, but applies in law to all legal modes of obtaining property except by inheritance or descent, and in this peculiar sense the word occurs five times in Shakespeare's thirty-four plays, and only in one single instance in the fifty-four plays of Beaumont and Fletcher. It has been suggested that it was in attendance upon the courts in London that he picked up his legal vocabulary. But this supposition not only fails to account for Shakespeare's peculiar freedom and exactness in the use of that phraseology, it does not even place him in the way of learning those terms his use of which is most remarkable, which are not such as he would have heard at ordinary proceedings at *nisi prius*, but such as refer to the tenure or transfer of real property, 'fine and recovery,' 'statutes merchant,' 'purchase,' 'indenture,' 'tenure,' 'double voucher,' 'fee simple,' 'fee farm,' 'remainder,' 'reversion,' 'forfeiture,' etc. This conveyancer's jargon could not have been picked up by hanging round the courts of law in London two hundred and fifty years ago, when suits as to the title of real property were comparatively rare. And beside, Shakespeare uses his law just as freely in his first plays, written in his first London years, as in those produced at a later period. Just as exactly, too; for the correctness and propriety with which these terms are introduced have compelled the admiration of a Chief Justice and a Lord Chancellor."

Senator Davis wrote: "We seem to have something more than a sciolist's temerity of indulgence in the terms of an unfamiliar art. No legal solecisms will be found. The abstrusest elements of the common law are impressed into a disciplined service. Over and over again, where such knowledge is unexampled in writers unlearned in the law, Shakespeare appears in perfect possession of it. In the law of real property, its rules of tenure and descents, its entails, its fines and recoveries, their vouchers and double vouchers, in the procedure of the Courts, the method of bringing writs and arrests, the nature of actions, the rules of pleading, the law of escapes and of contempt of court, in the principles of evidence, both technical and philosophical, in the distinction between the temporal and spiritual tribunals, in the law of attainder and forfeiture, in the requisites of a valid marriage, in the presumption of legitimacy, in the learning of the law of prerogative, in the inalienable character of the Crown, this mastership appears with surprising authority."

To all this testimony (and there is much more which I have not cited) may now be added that of a great lawyer of our own times, *viz.*: Sir James Plaisted Wilde, Q.C. created a Baron of the Exchequer in 1860, promoted to the post of Judge-Ordinary and Judge of the Courts of Probate and Divorce in 1863, and better known to the world as Lord Penzance, to which dignity he was raised in 1869. Lord Penzance, as all lawyers know, and as the late

Mr. Inderwick, K.C., has testified, was one of the first legal authorities of his day, famous for his "remarkable grasp of legal principles," and "endowed by nature with a remarkable facility for marshalling facts, and for a clear expression of his views."

Lord Penzance speaks of Shakespeare's "perfect familiarity with not only the principles, axioms, and maxims, but the technicalities of English law, a knowledge so perfect and intimate that he was never incorrect and never at fault . . . The mode in which this knowledge was pressed into service on all occasions to express his meaning and illustrate his thoughts, was quite unexampled. He seems to have had a special pleasure in his complete and ready mastership of it in all its branches. As manifested in the plays, this legal knowledge and learning had therefore a special character which places it on a wholly different footing from the rest of the multifarious knowledge which is exhibited in page after page of the plays. At every turn and point at which the author required a metaphor, simile, or illustration, his mind ever turned *first* to the law. He seems almost to have *thought* in legal phrases, the commonest of legal expressions were ever at the end of his pen in description or illustration. That he should have descanted in lawyer language when he had a forensic subject in hand, such as Shylock's bond, was to be expected, but the knowledge of law in 'Shakespeare' was exhibited in a far different manner: it protruded itself on all occasions, appropriate or inappropriate, and mingled itself with strains of thought widely divergent from forensic subjects." Again: "To acquire a perfect familiarity with legal principles, and an accurate and ready use of the technical terms and phrases not only of the conveyancer's office but of the pleader's chambers and the Courts at Westminster, nothing short of employment in some career involving constant contact with legal questions and general legal work would be requisite. But a continuous employment involves the element of time, and time was just what the manager of two theatres had not at his disposal. In what portion of Shakespeare's (*i.e.* Shakspere's) career would it be possible to point out that time could be found for the interposition of a legal employment in the chambers or offices of practising lawyers?"

Stratfordians, as is well known, casting about for some possible explanation of Shakespeare's extraordinary knowledge of law, have made the suggestion that Shakespeare might, conceivably, have been a clerk in an attorney's office before he came to London. Mr. Collier wrote to Lord Campbell to ask his opinion as to the probability of this being true. His answer was as follows: "You require us to believe implicitly a fact, of which, if true, positive and irrefragable evidence in his own handwriting might have been forthcoming to establish it. Not having been actually enrolled as an attorney, neither the records of the local court at Stratford nor of the superior Courts at Westminster would present his name as being concerned in any suit as an attorney, but it might reasonably have been expected that there would be deeds or wills witnessed by him still extant, and after a very diligent search none such can be discovered."

Upon this Lord Penzance comments: "It cannot be doubted that Lord Campbell was right in this. No young man could have been at work in an attorney's office without being called upon continually to act as a witness, and in many other ways leaving traces of his work and name." There is not a single fact or incident in all that is known of Shakespeare, even by rumor or tradition, which supports this notion of a clerkship. And after much argument and surmise which has been indulged in on this subject, we may, I think, safely put the notion on one side, for no less an authority than Mr. Grant White says finally that the idea of his having been clerk to an attorney has been "blown to pieces."

It is altogether characteristic of Mr. Churton Collins that he, nevertheless, adopts this exploded myth. "That Shakespeare was in early life employed as a clerk in an attorney's office, may be correct. At Stratford there was by royal charter a Court of Record sitting every fortnight, with six attorneys, beside the town clerk, belonging to it, and it is certainly not straining probability to suppose that the young Shakespeare may have had employment in one of them. There is, it is true, no tradition to this effect, but such traditions as we have about Shakespeare's occupation between the time of leaving school and going to London are so loose and baseless that no confidence can be placed in them. It is, to say the least, more probable that he was in an attorney's office than that he was a butcher killing calves 'in a high style,' and making speeches over them."

This is a charming specimen of Stratfordian argument. There is, as we have seen, a very old tradition that Shakespeare was a butcher's apprentice. John Dowdall, who made a tour in Warwickshire in 1693, testifies to it as coming from the old clerk who showed him over the church, and it is unhesitatingly accepted as true by Mr. Halliwell-Phillipps. (Vol I, p. 11, and see Vol. II, p.

71, 72.) Mr. Sidney Lee sees nothing improbable in it, and it is supported by Aubrey, who must have written his account some time before 1680, when his manuscript was completed. Of the attorney's clerk hypothesis, on the other hand, there is not the faintest vestige of a tradition. It has been evolved out of the fertile imaginations of embarrassed Stratfordians, seeking for some explanation of the Stratford rustic's marvellous acquaintance with law and legal terms and legal life. But Mr. Churton Collins has not the least hesitation in throwing over the tradition which has the warrant of antiquity and setting up in its stead this ridiculous invention, for which not only is there no shred of positive evidence, but which, as Lord Campbell and Lord Penzance point out, is really put out of court by the negative evidence, since "no young man could have been at work in an attorney's office without being called upon continually to act as a witness, and in many other ways leaving traces of his work and name." And as Mr. Edwards further points out, since the day when Lord Campbell's book was published (between forty and fifty years ago), "every old deed or will, to say nothing of other legal papers, dated during the period of William Shakespeare's youth, has been scrutinized over half a dozen shires, and not one signature of the young man has been found."

Moreover, if Shakespeare had served as clerk in an attorney's office it is clear that he must have so served for a considerable period in order to have gained (if indeed it is credible that he could have so gained) his remarkable knowledge of law. Can we then for a moment believe that, if this had been so, tradition would have been absolutely silent on the matter? That Dowdall's old clerk, over eighty years of age, should have never heard of it (though he was sure enough about the butcher's apprentice), and that all the other ancient witnesses should be in similar ignorance!

But such are the methods of Stratfordian controversy. Tradition is to be scouted when it is found inconvenient, but cited as irrefragable truth when it suits the case. Shakespeare of Stratford was the author of the *Plays* and *Poems*, but the author of the *Plays* and *Poems* could not have been a butcher's apprentice. Away, therefore, with tradition. But the author of the *Plays* and *Poems* *must* have had a very large and a very accurate knowledge of the law. Therefore, Shakespeare of Stratford must have been an attorney's clerk! The method is simplicity itself. By similar reasoning Shakespeare has been made a country schoolmaster, a soldier, a physician, a printer, and a good many other things beside, according to the inclination and the exigencies of the commentator. It would not be in the least surprising to find that he was studying Latin as a schoolmaster and law in an attorney's office at the same time.

However, we must do Mr. Collins the justice of saying that he has fully recognized, what is indeed tolerably obvious, that Shakespeare must have had a sound legal training. "It may, of course, be urged," he writes, "that Shakespeare's knowledge of medicine, and particularly that branch of it which related to morbid psychology, is equally remarkable, and that no one has ever contended that he was a physician. (Here Mr. Collins is wrong; that contention also has been put forward.) It may be urged that his acquaintance with the technicalities of other crafts and callings, notably of marine and military affairs, was also extraordinary, and yet no one has suspected him of being a sailor or a soldier. (Wrong again. Why even Messrs. Garnett and Gosse 'suspect' that he was a soldier!) This may be conceded, but the concession hardly furnishes an analogy. To these and all other subjects he recurs occasionally, and in season, but with reminiscences of the law his memory, as is abundantly clear, was simply saturated. In season and out of season now in manifest, now in recondite application, he presses it into the service of expression and illustration. At least a third of his myriad metaphors are derived from it. It would indeed be difficult to find a single act in any of his dramas, nay, in some of them, a single scene, the diction and imagery of which is not colored by it. Much of his law may have been acquired from three books easily accessible to him, namely Tottell's *Precedents* (1572), Pulton's *Statutes* (1578), and Fraunce's *Lawier's Logike* (1588), works with which he certainly seems to have been familiar; but much of it could only have come from one who had an intimate acquaintance with legal proceedings. We quite agree with Mr. Castle that Shakespeare's legal knowledge is not what could have been picked up in an attorney's office, but could only have been learned by an actual attendance at the Courts, at a Pleader's Chambers, and on circuit, or by associating intimately with members of the Bench and Bar."

This is excellent. But what is Mr. Collins' explanation. "Perhaps the simplest solution of the problem is to accept the hypothesis that in early life he was in an attorney's office (!), that he there contracted a love for the law which never left him, that as a young man in London, he continued to study or dabble in it for his amusement, to stroll in leisure hours into the Courts, and to frequent the society of lawyers. On no other supposition is it possible to explain the attraction which the law evidently had for him, and his minute and undeviating accuracy in a subject where no layman who has indulged in such copious and ostentatious display of legal technicalities has ever yet succeeded in keeping himself from tripping."

A lame conclusion. "No other supposition" indeed! Yes, there is another, and a very obvious supposition, namely, that Shakespeare was himself a lawyer, well versed in his trade, versed in all the ways of the courts, and living in close intimacy with judges and members of the Inns of Court.

One is, of course, thankful that Mr. Collins has appreciated the fact that Shakespeare must have had a sound legal training, but I may be forgiven if I do not attach quite so much importance to his pronouncements on this branch of the subject as to those of Malone, Lord Campbell, Judge Holmes, Mr. Castle, K.C., Lord Penzance, Mr. Grant White, and other lawyers, who have expressed their opinion on the matter of Shakespeare's legal acquirements.

Here it may, perhaps, be worth while to quote again from Lord Penzance's book as to the suggestion that Shakespeare had somehow or other managed "to acquire a perfect familiarity with legal principles, and an accurate and ready use of the technical terms and phrases, not only of the conveyancer's office, but of the pleader's chambers and the courts at Westminster." This, as Lord Penzance points out, "would require nothing short of employment in some career involving *constant contact* with legal questions and general legal work." But "in what portion of Shakespeare's career would it be possible to point out that time could be found for the interposition of a legal employment in the chambers or offices of practising lawyers? . . . It is beyond doubt that at an early period he was called upon to abandon his attendance at school and assist his father, and was soon after, at the age of sixteen, bound apprentice to a trade. While under the obligation of this bond he could not have pursued any other employment. Then he leaves Stratford and comes to London. He has to provide himself with the means of a livelihood, and this he did in some capacity at the theatre. No one doubts that. The holding of horses is scouted by many, and perhaps with justice, as being unlikely and certainly unproved; but whatever the nature of his employment was at the theatre, there is hardly room for the belief that it could have been other than continuous, for his progress there was so rapid. Ere long he had been taken into the company as an actor, and was soon spoken of as a 'Johannes Factotum.' His rapid accumulation of wealth speaks volumes for the constancy and activity of his services. One fails to see when there could be a break in the current of his life at this period of it, giving room or opportunity for legal or indeed any other employment. 'In 1589,' says Knight, 'we have undeniable evidence that he had not only a casual engagement, was not only a salaried servant, as many players were, but was a shareholder in the company of the Queen's players with other shareholders below him on the list.' This (1589) would be within two years after his arrival in London, which is placed by White and Halliwell-Phillipps about the year 1587. The difficulty in supposing that, starting with a state of ignorance in 1587, when he is supposed to have come to London, he was induced to enter upon a course of most extended study and mental culture, is almost insuperable. Still it was physically possible, provided always that he could have had access to the needful books. But this legal training seems to me to stand on a different footing. It is not only unaccountable and incredible, but it is actually negatived by the known facts of his career." Lord Penzance then refers to the fact that "by 1592 (according to the best authority, Mr. Grant White) several of the plays had been written. *The Comedy of Errors* in 1589, *Love's Labour's Lost* in 1589, *Two Gentlemen of Verona* in 1589 or 1590, and so forth," and then asks, "with this catalogue of dramatic work on hand . . . was it possible that he could have taken a leading part in the management and conduct of two theatres, and if Mr. Phillipps is to be relied upon, taken his share in the performances of the provincial tours of his company—and at the same time devoted himself to the study of the law in all its branches so efficiently as to make himself complete master of its principles and practice, and saturate his mind with all its most technical terms?"

I have cited this passage from Lord Penzance's book, because it lay before me, and I had already quoted from it on the matter of Shakespeare's legal knowledge; but other writers have still better set forth the insuperable difficulties, as they seem to me, which beset the idea that Shakespeare might have found time in some unknown period of early life, amid multifarious other occupations, for the study of classics, literature and law, to say nothing of languages and a few other matters. Lord Penzance further asks his readers: "Did you ever meet with or hear of an instance in which a young man in this country gave himself up to legal studies and engaged in legal employments, which is the only way of becoming familiar with the technicalities of practice, unless with the view of practicing in that profession? I do not believe that it would be easy, or indeed possible, to produce an instance in which the law has been seriously studied in all its branches, except as a qualification for practice in the legal profession."

* * * * *

This testimony is so strong, so direct, so authoritative; and so uncheapened, unwatered by guesses, and surmises, and maybe-so's, and might-have-beens, and could-have-beens, and must-have-beens, and the rest of that ton of plaster of paris out of which the biographers have built the colossal brontosaur which goes by the Stratford actor's name, that it quite convinces me that the man who wrote Shakespeare's Works knew all about law and lawyers. Also, that that man could not have been the Stratford Shakespeare—and *wasn't*.

Who did write these Works, then?

I wish I knew.

CHAPTER IX

Did Francis Bacon write Shakespeare's Works?

Nobody knows.

We cannot say we *know* a thing when that thing has not been proved. *Know* is too strong a word to use when the evidence is not final and absolutely conclusive. We can infer, if we want to, like those slaves . . . No, I will not write that word, it is not kind, it is not courteous. The upholders of the Stratford-Shakespeare superstition call *us* the hardest names they can think of, and they keep doing it all the time; very well, if they like to descend to that level, let them do it, but I will not so undignify myself as to follow them. I cannot call them harsh names; the most I can do is to indicate them by terms reflecting my disapproval; and this without malice, without venom.

To resume. What I was about to say, was, those thugs have built their entire superstition upon *inferences*, not upon known and established facts. It is a weak method, and poor, and I am glad to be able to say our side never resorts to it while there is anything else to resort to.

But when we must, we must; and we have now arrived at a place of that sort.

Since the Stratford Shakespeare couldn't have written the Works, we infer that somebody did. Who was it, then? This requires some more inferring.

Ordinarily when an unsigned poem sweeps across the continent like a tidal wave, whose roar and boom and thunder are made up of admiration, delight and applause, a dozen obscure people rise up and claim the authorship. Why a dozen, instead of only one or two? One reason is, because there's a dozen that are recognizably competent to do that poem. Do you remember "Beautiful Snow"? Do you remember "Rock Me to Sleep, Mother, Rock Me to Sleep"? Do you remember "Backward, turn backward, O Time, in thy flight! Make me a child again just for to-night"? I remember them very well. Their authorship was claimed by most of the grown-up people who were alive at the time, and every claimant had one plausible argument in his favor, at least: to wit, he could have done the authoring; he was competent.

Have the Works been claimed by a dozen? They haven't. There was good reason. The world knows there was but one man on the planet at the time who was competent—not a dozen, and not two. A long time ago the dwellers in a far country used now and then to find a procession of prodigious footprints stretching across the plain—footprints that were three miles apart, each footprint a third of a mile long and a furlong deep, and with forests and villages mashed to mush in it. Was there any doubt as to who had made that mighty trail? Were there a dozen claimants? Were there two? No—the people knew who it was that had been along there: there was only one Hercules.

There has been only one Shakespeare. There couldn't be two; certainly there couldn't be two at the same time. It takes ages to bring forth a Shakespeare, and some more ages to match him. This one was not matched before his time; nor during his time; and hasn't been matched since. The prospect of matching him in our time is not bright.

The Baconians claim that the Stratford Shakespeare was not qualified to write the Works, and that Francis Bacon was. They claim that Bacon possessed the stupendous equipment—both natural and acquired—for the miracle; and that no other Englishman of his day possessed the like; or, indeed, anything closely approaching it.

Macaulay, in his Essay, has much to say about the splendor and horizonless magnitude of that equipment. Also, he has synopsized Bacon's history: a thing which cannot be done for the Stratford Shakespeare, for he hasn't any history to synopsize. Bacon's history is open to the world, from his boyhood to his death in old age—a history consisting of known facts, displayed in minute and multitudinous detail; *facts*, not guesses and conjectures and might-have-beens.

Whereby it appears that he was born of a race of statesmen, and had a Lord Chancellor for his father, and a mother who was "distinguished both as a linguist and a theologian: she corresponded in Greek with Bishop Jewell, and translated his *Apologia* from the Latin so correctly that neither he nor Archbishop Parker could suggest a single alteration." It is the atmosphere we are reared in that determines how our inclinations and aspirations shall tend. The atmosphere furnished by the parents to the son in this present case was an atmosphere saturated with learning; with thinkings and ponderings upon deep subjects; and with polite culture. It had its natural effect. Shakespeare of Stratford was reared in a house which had no use for books, since its owners, his parents, were without education. This may have had an effect upon the son, but we do not know, because we have no history of him of an informing sort. There were but few books anywhere, in that day, and only the well-to-do and highly educated possessed them, they being almost confined to the dead languages. "All the valuable books then extant in all the vernacular dialects of Europe would hardly have filled a single shelf"— imagine it! The few existing books were in the Latin tongue mainly. "A person who was ignorant of it was shut out from all acquaintance—not merely with Cicero and Virgil, but with the most interesting memoirs, state papers, and pamphlets of his own time"—a literature necessary to the Stratford lad, for his fictitious reputation's sake, since the writer of his Works would begin to use it wholesale and in a most masterly way before the lad was hardly more than out of his teens and into his twenties.

At fifteen Bacon was sent to the university, and he spent three years there. Thence he went to Paris in the train of the English Ambassador, and there he mingled daily with the wise, the cultured, the great, and the aristocracy of fashion, during another three years. A total of six years spent at the sources of knowledge; knowledge both of books and of men. The three spent at the university were coeval with the second and last three spent by the little Stratford lad at Stratford school supposedly, and perhapsedly, and maybe, and by inference—with nothing to infer from. The second three of the Baconian six were "presumably" spent by the Stratford lad as apprentice to a butcher. That is, the thugs presume it—on no evidence of any kind. Which is their way, when they want a historical fact. Fact and presumption are, for business purposes, all the same to them. They know the difference, but they also know how to blink it. They know, too, that while in history-building a fact is better than a presumption, it doesn't take a presumption long to bloom into a fact when *they* have the handling of it. They know by old experience that when they get hold of a presumption-tadpole he is not going to *stay* tadpole in their history-tank; no, they know how to develop him into the giant four-legged bullfrog of *fact*, and make him sit up on his hams, and puff out his chin, and look important and insolent and come-to-stay; and assert his genuine simon-pure authenticity with a thundering bellow that will convince everybody because it is so loud. The thug is aware that loudness convinces sixty persons where reasoning convinces but one. I wouldn't be a thug, not even if—but never mind about that, it has nothing to do with the argument, and it is not noble in spirit besides. If I am better than a thug, is the merit mine? No, it is His. Then to Him be the praise. That is the right spirit.

They "presume" the lad severed his "presumed" connection with the Stratford school to become apprentice to a butcher. They also "presume" that the butcher was his father. They don't know. There is no written record of it, nor any other actual evidence. If it would have helped their case any, they would have apprenticed him to thirty butchers, to fifty butchers, to a wilderness of butchers—all by their patented method "presumption." If it will help their case they will do it yet; and if it will further help it, they will "presume" that all those butchers were his father. And the week after, they will *say* it. Why, it is just like being the past tense of the compound reflexive adverbial incandescent hypodermic irregular accusative Noun of Multitude; which is father to the expression which the grammarians call Verb. It is like a whole ancestry, with only one posterity.

To resume. Next, the young Bacon took up the study of law, and mastered that abstruse science. From that day to the end of his life he was daily in close contact with lawyers and judges; not as a casual onlooker in intervals between holding horses in front of a theatre, but as a practicing lawyer—a great and successful one, a renowned one, a Launcelot of the bar, the most formidable lance in the high brotherhood of the legal Table Round; he lived in the law's atmosphere thenceforth, all his years, and by sheer ability forced his way up its difficult steeps to its supremest summit, the Lord Chancellorship, leaving behind him no fellow craftsman qualified to challenge his divine right to that majestic place.

When we read the praises bestowed by Lord Penzance and the other illustrious experts upon the legal condition and legal aptnesses, brilliances, profundities and felicities so prodigally displayed in the Plays, and try to fit them to the history-less Stratford stage-manager, they sound wild, strange, incredible, ludicrous; but when we put them in the mouth of Bacon they do not sound strange, they seem in their natural and rightful place, they seem at home there. Please turn back and read them again. Attributed to Shakespeare of Stratford they are meaningless, they are inebriate extravagancies—intemperate admirations of the dark side of the moon, so to speak; attributed to Bacon, they are admirations of the golden glories of the moon's front side, the moon at the full—and not intemperate, not overwrought, but sane and right, and justified. "At every turn and point at which the author required a metaphor, simile or illustration, his mind ever turned *first* to the law; he seems almost to have *thought* in legal phrases; the commonest legal phrases, the commonest of legal expressions were ever at the end of his pen." That could happen to no one but a person whose *trade* was the law; it could not happen to a dabbler in it. Veteran mariners fill their conversation with sailor-phrases and draw all their similes from the ship and the sea and the storm, but no mere *passenger* ever does it, be he of Stratford or elsewhere; or could do it with anything resembling accuracy, if he were hardy enough to try. Please read again what Lord Campbell and the other great authorities have said about Bacon when they thought they were saying it about Shakespeare of Stratford.

Is Shakespeare Dead?

CHAPTER X

The Rest of the Equipment

The author of the Plays was equipped, beyond every other man of his time, with wisdom, erudition, imagination, capaciousness of mind, grace and majesty of expression. Every one has said it, no one doubts it. Also, he had humor, humor in rich abundance, and always wanting to break out. We have no evidence of any kind that Shakespeare of Stratford possessed any of these gifts or any of these acquirements. The only lines he ever wrote, so far as we know, are substantially barren of them—barren of all of them.

> *Good friend for Iesus sake forbeare*
> *To digg the dust encloased heare:*
> *Blest be ye man yt spares thes stones*
> *And curst be he yt moves my bones.*

Ben Jonson says of Bacon, as orator:

His language, *where he could spare and pass by a jest*, was nobly censorious. No man ever spoke more neatly, more pressly, more weightily, or suffered less emptiness, less idleness, in what he uttered. No member of his speech but consisted of his (its) own graces . . . The fear of every man that heard him was lest he should make an end.

From Macaulay:

He continued to distinguish himself in Parliament, particularly by his exertions in favor of one excellent measure on which the King's heart was set—the union of England and Scotland. It was not difficult for such an intellect to discover many irresistible arguments in favor of such a scheme. He conducted the great case of the *Post Nati* in the Exchequer Chamber; and the decision of the judges—a decision the legality of which may be questioned, but the beneficial effect of which must be acknowledged—was in a great measure attributed to his dexterous management.

Again:

While actively engaged in the House of Commons and in the courts of law, he still found leisure for letters and philosophy. The noble treatise on the *Advancement of Learning*, which at a later period was expanded into the *De Augmentis*, appeared in 1605.

The *Wisdom of the Ancients*, a work which if it had proceeded from any other writer would have been considered as a masterpiece of wit and learning, was printed in 1609.

In the meantime the *Novum Organum* was slowly proceeding. Several distinguished men of learning had been permitted to see portions of that extraordinary book, and they spoke with the greatest admiration of his genius.

Even Sir Thomas Bodley, after perusing the *Cogitata et Visa*, one of the most precious of those scattered leaves out of which the great oracular volume was afterward made up, acknowledged that "in all proposals and plots in that book, Bacon showed himself a master workman"; and that "it could not be gainsaid but all the treatise over did abound with choice conceits of the present state of learning, and with worthy contemplations of the means to procure it."

In 1612 a new edition of the *Essays* appeared, with additions surpassing the original collection both in bulk and quality.

Nor did these pursuits distract Bacon's attention from a work the most arduous, the most glorious, and the most useful that even his mighty powers could have achieved, "the reducing and recompiling," to use his own phrase, "of the laws of England."

To serve the exacting and laborious offices of Attorney General and Solicitor General would have satisfied the appetite of any other man for hard work, but Bacon had to add the vast literary industries just described, to satisfy his. He was a born worker.

The service which he rendered to letters during the last five years of his life, amid ten thousand distractions and vexations, increase the regret with which we think on the many years which he had wasted, to use the words of Sir Thomas Bodley, "on such study as was not worthy such a student."

He commenced a digest of the laws of England, a History of England under the Princes of the House of Tudor, a body of National History, a Philosophical Romance. He made extensive and valuable additions to his Essays. He published the inestimable *Treatise De Argumentis Scientiarum*.

Did these labors of Hercules fill up his time to his contentment, and quiet his appetite for work? Not entirely:

The trifles with which he amused himself in hours of pain and languor bore the mark of his mind. *The best jestbook in the world* is that which he dictated from memory, without referring to any book, on a day on which illness had rendered him incapable of serious study.

Here are some scattered remarks (from Macaulay) which throw light upon Bacon, and seem to indicate—and maybe demonstrate—that he was competent to write the Plays and Poems:

With great minuteness of observation he had an amplitude of comprehension such as has never yet been vouchsafed to any other human being.

The "Essays" contain abundant proofs that no nice feature of character, no peculiarity in the ordering of a house, a garden or a court-masque, could escape the notice of one whose mind was capable of taking in the whole world of knowledge.

His understanding resembled the tent which the fairy Paribanou gave to Prince Ahmed: fold it, and it seemed a toy for the hand of a lady; spread it, and the armies of powerful Sultans might repose beneath its shade.

The knowledge in which Bacon excelled all men was a knowledge of the mutual relations of all departments of knowledge.

In a letter written when he was only thirty-one, to his uncle, Lord Burleigh, he said, "I have taken all knowledge to be my province."

Though Bacon did not arm his philosophy with the weapons of logic, he adorned her profusely with all the richest decorations of rhetoric.

The practical faculty was powerful in Bacon; but not, like his wit, so powerful as occasionally to usurp the place of his reason, and to tyrannize over the whole man.

There are too many places in the Plays where this happens. Poor old dying John of Gaunt volleying second-rate puns at his own name, is a pathetic instance of it. "We may assume" that it is Bacon's fault, but the Stratford Shakespeare has to bear the blame.

No imagination was ever at once so strong and so thoroughly subjugated. It stopped at the first check from good sense.

In truth much of Bacon's life was passed in a visionary world—amid things as strange as any that are described in the "Arabian Tales" . . . amid buildings more sumptuous than the palace of Aladdin, fountains more wonderful than the golden water of Parizade, conveyances more rapid than the hippogryph of Ruggiero, arms more formidable than the lance of Astolfo, remedies more efficacious than the balsam of Fierabras. Yet in his magnificent day-dreams there was nothing wild—nothing but what sober reason sanctioned.

Bacon's greatest performance is the first book of the *Novum Organum* . . . Every part of it blazes with wit, but with wit which is employed only to illustrate and decorate truth. No book ever made so great a revolution in the mode of thinking, overthrew so many prejudices, introduced so many new opinions.

But what we most admire is the vast capacity of that intellect which, without effort, takes in at once all the domains of science—all the past, the present and the future, all the errors of two thousand years, all the encouraging signs of the passing times, all the bright hopes of the coming age.

He had a wonderful talent for packing thought close and rendering it portable.

Mark Twain

His eloquence would alone have entitled him to a high rank in literature.

It is evident that he had each and every one of the mental gifts and each and every one of the acquirements that are so prodigally displayed in the Plays and Poems, and in much higher and richer degree than any other man of his time or of any previous time. He was a genius without a mate, a prodigy not matable. There was only one of him; the planet could not produce two of him at one birth, nor in one age. He could have written anything that is in the Plays and Poems. He could have written this:

> *The cloud-cap'd towers,*
> *the gorgeous palaces,*
> *The solemn temples,*
> *the great globe itself,*
>
> *Yea, all which it inherit,*
> *shall dissolve,*

And, like an insubstantial pageant faded,

> *Leave not a rack behind.*
> *We are such stuff*
> *As dreams are made on,*
> *and our little life*
> *Is rounded with a sleep.*

Also, he could have written this, but he refrained:

> *Good friend for Iesus sake forbeare*
> *To digg the dust encloased heare:*
> *Blest be ye man yt spares thes stones*
> *And curst be ye yt moves my bones.*

When a person reads the noble verses about the cloud-cap'd towers, he ought not to follow it immediately with Good friend for Iesus sake forbeare, because he will find the transition from great poetry to poor prose too violent for comfort. It will give him a shock. You never notice how commonplace and unpoetic gravel is, until you bite into a layer of it in a pie.

Is Shakespeare Dead?

CHAPTER XI

Am I trying to convince anybody that Shakespeare did not write Shakespeare's Works? Ah, now, what do you take me for? Would I be so soft as that, after having known the human race familiarly for nearly seventy-four years? It would grieve me to know that any one could think so injuriously of me, so uncomplimentarily, so unadmiringly of me. No-no, I am aware that when even the brightest mind in our world has been trained up from childhood in a superstition of any kind, it will never be possible for that mind, in its maturity, to examine sincerely, dispassionately, and conscientiously any evidence or any circumstance which shall seem to cast a doubt upon the validity of that superstition. I doubt if I could do it myself. We always get at second hand our notions about systems of government; and high-tariff and low-tariff; and prohibition and anti-prohibition; and the holiness of peace and the glories of war; and codes of honor and codes of morals; and approval of the duel and disapproval of it; and our beliefs concerning the nature of cats; and our ideas as to whether the murder of helpless wild animals is base or is heroic; and our preferences in the matter of religious and political parties; and our acceptance or rejection of the Shakespeares and the Arthur Ortons and the Mrs. Eddys. We get them all at second-hand, we reason none of them out for ourselves. It is the way we are made. It is the way we are all made, and we can't help it, we can't change it. And whenever we have been furnished a fetish, and have been taught to believe in it, and love it and worship it, and refrain from examining it, there is no evidence, howsoever clear and strong, that can persuade us to withdraw from it our loyalty and our devotion. In morals, conduct, and beliefs we take the color of our environment and associations, and it is a color that can safely be warranted to wash. Whenever we have been furnished with a tar baby ostensibly stuffed with jewels, and warned that it will be dishonorable and irreverent to disembowel it and test the jewels, we keep our sacrilegious hands off it. We submit, not reluctantly, but rather gladly, for we are privately afraid we should find, upon examination, that the jewels are of the sort that are manufactured at North Adams, Mass.

I haven't any idea that Shakespeare will have to vacate his pedestal this side of the year 2209. Disbelief in him cannot come swiftly, disbelief in a healthy and deeply-loved tar baby has never been known to disintegrate swiftly, it is a very slow process. It took several thousand years to convince our fine race—including every splendid intellect in it—that there is no such thing as a witch; it has taken several thousand years to convince that same fine race—including every splendid intellect in it—that there is no such person as Satan; it has taken several centuries to remove perdition from the Protestant Church's program of postmortem entertainments; it has taken a weary long time to persuade American Presbyterians to give up infant damnation and try to bear it the best they can; and it looks as if their Scotch brethren will still be burning babies in the everlasting fires when Shakespeare comes down from his perch.

We are The Reasoning Race. We can't prove it by the above examples, and we can't prove it by the miraculous "histories" built by those Stratfordolaters out of a hatful of rags and a barrel of sawdust, but there is a plenty of other things we can prove it by, if I could think of them. We are The Reasoning Race, and when we find a vague file of chipmunk-tracks stringing through the dust of Stratford village, we know by our reasoning powers that Hercules has been along there. I feel that our fetish is safe for three centuries yet. The bust, too—there in the Stratford Church. The precious bust, the priceless bust, the calm bust, the serene bust, the emotionless bust, with the dandy moustache, and the putty face, unseamed of care—that face which has looked passionlessly down upon the awed pilgrim for a hundred and fifty years and will still look down upon the awed pilgrim three hundred more, with the deep, deep, deep, subtle, subtle, subtle, expression of a bladder.

CHAPTER XII

Irreverence

One of the most trying defects which I find in these—these—what shall I call them? for I will not apply injurious epithets to them, the way they do to us, such violations of courtesy being repugnant to my nature and my dignity. The furthest I can go in that direction is to call them by names of limited reverence—names merely descriptive, never unkind, never offensive, never tainted by harsh feeling. If *they* would do like this, they would feel better in their hearts. Very well, then—to proceed. One of the most trying defects which I find in these Stratfordolaters, these Shakesperoids, these thugs, these bangalores, these troglodytes, these herumfrodites, these blatherskites, these buccaneers, these bandoleers, is their spirit of irreverence. It is detectable in every utterance of theirs when they are talking about us. I am thankful that in me there is nothing of that spirit. When a thing is sacred to me it is impossible for me to be irreverent toward it. I cannot call to mind a single instance where I have ever been irreverent, except toward the things which were sacred to other people. Am I in the right? I think so. But I ask no one to take my unsupported word; no, look at the dictionary; let the dictionary decide. Here is the definition:

Irreverence. The quality or condition of irreverence toward God and sacred things.

What does the Hindu say? He says it is correct. He says irreverence is lack of respect for Vishnu, and Brahma, and Chrishna, and his other gods, and for his sacred cattle, and for his temples and the things within them. He endorses the definition, you see; and there are 300,000,000 Hindus or their equivalents back of him.

The dictionary had the acute idea that by using the capital G it could restrict irreverence to lack of reverence for *our* Deity and our sacred things, but that ingenious and rather sly idea miscarried: for by the simple process of spelling *his* deities with capitals the Hindu confiscates the definition and restricts it to his own sects, thus making it clearly compulsory upon us to revere *his* gods and *his* sacred things, and nobody's else. We can't say a word, for he has our own dictionary at his back, and its decision is final.

This law, reduced to its simplest terms, is this: 1. Whatever is sacred to the Christian must be held in reverence by everybody else; 2, whatever is sacred to the Hindu must be held in reverence by everybody else; 3, therefore, by consequence, logically, and indisputably, whatever is sacred to *me* must be held in reverence by everybody else.

Now then, what aggravates me is, that these troglodytes and muscovites and bandoleers and buccaneers are *also* trying to crowd in and share the benefit of the law, and compel everybody to revere their Shakespeare and hold him sacred. We can't have that: there's enough of us already. If you go on widening and spreading and inflating the privilege, it will presently come to be conceded that each man's sacred things are the *only* ones, and the rest of the human race will have to be humbly reverent toward them or suffer for it. That can surely happen, and when it happens, the word Irreverence will be regarded as the most meaningless, and foolish, and self-conceited, and insolent, and impudent and dictatorial word in the language. And people will say, "Whose business is it, what gods I worship and what things hold sacred? Who has the right to dictate to my conscience, and where did he get that right?"

We cannot afford to let that calamity come upon us. We must save the word from this destruction. There is but one way to do it, and that is, to stop the spread of the privilege, and strictly confine it to its present limits: that is, to all the Christian sects, to all the Hindu sects, and me. We do not need any more, the stock is watered enough, just as it is.

It would be better if the privilege were limited to me alone. I think so because I am the only sect that knows how to employ it gently, kindly, charitably, dispassionately. The other sects lack the quality of self-restraint.

Mark Twain

The Catholic Church says the most irreverent things about matters which are sacred to the Protestants, and the Protestant Church retorts in kind about the confessional and other matters which Catholics hold sacred; then both of these irreverencers turn upon Thomas Paine and charge *him* with irreverence. This is all unfortunate, because it makes it difficult for students equipped with only a low grade of mentality to find out what Irreverence really *is*.

It will surely be much better all around if the privilege of regulating the irreverent and keeping them in order shall eventually be withdrawn from all the sects but me. Then there will be no more quarrelling, no more bandying of disrespectful epithets, no more heart burnings.

There will then be nothing sacred involved in this Bacon-Shakespeare controversy except what is sacred to me. That will simplify the whole matter, and trouble will cease. There will be irreverence no longer, because I will not allow it. The first time those criminals charge me with irreverence for calling their Stratford myth an Arthur-Orton-Mary-Baker-Thompson-Eddy-Louis-the-Seventeenth-Veiled-Prophet-of-Khorassan will be the last. Taught by the methods found effective in extinguishing earlier offenders by the Inquisition, of holy memory, I shall know how to quiet them.

Is Shakespeare Dead?

CHAPTER XIII

Isn't it odd, when you think of it: that you may list all the celebrated Englishmen, Irishmen, and Scotchmen of modern times, clear back to the first Tudors—a list containing five hundred names, shall we say?—and you can go to the histories, biographies and cyclopedias and learn the particulars of the lives of every one of them. Every one of them except one—the most famous, the most renowned—by far the most illustrious of them all— Shakespeare! You can get the details of the lives of all the celebrated ecclesiastics in the list; all the celebrated tragedians, comedians, singers, dancers, orators, judges, lawyers, poets, dramatists, historians, biographers, editors, inventors, reformers, statesmen, generals, admirals, discoverers, prize-fighters, murderers, pirates, conspirators, horse-jockeys, bunco-steerers, misers, swindlers, explorers, adventurers by land and sea, bankers, financiers, astronomers, naturalists, Claimants, impostors, chemists, biologists, geologists, philologists, college presidents and professors, architects, engineers, painters, sculptors, politicians, agitators, rebels, revolutionists, patriots, demagogues, clowns, cooks, freaks, philosophers, burglars, highwaymen, journalists, physicians, surgeons—you can get the life-histories of all of them but *one*. Just one—the most extraordinary and the most celebrated of them all—Shakespeare!

You may add to the list the thousand celebrated persons furnished by the rest of Christendom in the past four centuries, and you can find out the life-histories of all those people, too. You will then have listed 1500 celebrities, and you can trace the authentic life-histories of the whole of them. Save one—far and away the most colossal prodigy of the entire accumulation— Shakespeare! About him you can find out *nothing*. Nothing of even the slightest importance. Nothing worth the trouble of stowing away in your memory. Nothing that even remotely indicates that he was ever anything more than a distinctly common-place person—a manager, an actor of inferior grade, a small trader in a small village that did not regard him as a person of any consequence, and had forgotten all about him before he was fairly cold in his grave. We can go to the records and find out the life-history of every renowned *race-horse* of modern times—but not Shakespeare's! There are many reasons why, and they have been furnished in cartloads (of guess and conjecture) by those troglodytes; but there is one that is worth all the rest of the reasons put together, and is abundantly sufficient all by itself—*he hadn't any history to record.* There is no way of getting around that deadly fact. And no sane way has yet been discovered of getting around its formidable significance.

Its quite plain significance—to any but those thugs (I do not use the term unkindly) is, that Shakespeare had no prominence while he lived, and none until he had been dead two or three generations. The Plays enjoyed high fame from the beginning; and if he wrote them it seems a pity the world did not find it out. He ought to have explained that he was the author, and not merely a *nom de plume* for another man to hide behind. If he had been less intemperately solicitous about his bones, and more solicitous about his Works, it would have been better for his good name, and a kindness to us. The bones were not important. They will moulder away, they will turn to dust, but the Works will endure until the last sun goes down.

Mark Twain.

P.S. *March* 25. About two months ago I was illuminating this Autobiography with some notions of mine concerning the Bacon-Shakespeare controversy, and I then took occasion to air the opinion that the Stratford Shakespeare was a person of no public consequence or celebrity during his lifetime, but was utterly obscure and unimportant. And not only in great London, but also in the little village where he was born, where he lived a quarter of a century, and where he died and was buried. I argued that if he had been a person of any note at all, aged villagers would have had much to tell about him many and many a year after his death, instead of being unable to furnish inquirers a single fact connected with him. I believed, and I still believe, that if he had been famous, his notoriety would have lasted as long as mine has lasted in my native village out in Missouri. It is a good argument, a prodigiously strong one, and a most formidable one for even the most gifted, and ingenious, and plausible Stratfordolater to get around or explain away. To-day a Hannibal *Courier-Post* of recent date has reached me, with an article in it which reinforces my contention that a really celebrated person cannot be forgotten in his village in the short space of sixty years. I will make an extract from it:

Hannibal, as a city, may have many sins to answer for, but ingratitude is not one of them, or reverence for the great men she has produced, and as the years go by her greatest son Mark Twain, or S. L. Clemens as a few of the unlettered call him, grows in the estimation and regard of the residents of the town he made famous and the town that made him famous. His name is associated with every old building that is torn down to make way for the modern structures demanded by a rapidly growing city, and with every hill or cave over or through which he might by any possibility have roamed, while the many points of interest which he wove into his stories, such as Holiday Hill, Jackson's Island, or Mark Twain Cave, are now monuments to his genius. Hannibal is glad of any opportunity to do him honor as he has honored her.

So it has happened that the "old timers" who went to school with Mark or were with him on some of his usual escapades have been honored with large audiences whenever they were in a reminiscent mood and condescended to tell of their intimacy with the ordinary boy who came to be a very extraordinary humorist and whose every boyish act is now seen to have been indicative of what was to come. Like Aunt Beckey and Mrs. Clemens, they can now see that Mark was hardly appreciated when he lived here and that the things he did as a boy and was whipped for doing were not all bad after all. So they have been in no hesitancy about drawing out the bad things he did as well as the good in their efforts to get a "Mark Twain story," all incidents being viewed in the light of his present fame, until the volume of "Twainiana" is already considerable and growing in proportion as the "old timers" drop away and the stories are retold second and third hand by their descendants. With some seventy-three years young and living in a villa instead of a house he is a fair target, and let him incorporate, copyright, or patent himself as he will, there are some of his "works" that will go swooping up Hannibal chimneys as long as gray-beards gather about the fires and begin with "I've heard father tell" or possibly "Once when I."

The Mrs. Clemens referred to is my mother—*was* my mother.

And here is another extract from a Hannibal paper. Of date twenty days ago:

Miss Becca Blankenship died at the home of William Dickason, 408 Rock Street, at 2.30 o'clock yesterday afternoon, aged 72 years. The deceased was a sister of "Huckleberry Finn," one of the famous characters in Mark Twain's *Tom Sawyer*. She had been a member of the Dickason family—the housekeeper—for nearly forty-five years, and was a highly respected lady. For the past eight years she had been an invalid, but was as well cared for by Mr. Dickason and his family as if she had been a near relative. She was a member of the Park Methodist Church and a Christian woman.

I remember her well. I have a picture of her in my mind which was graven there, clear and sharp and vivid, sixty-three years ago. She was at that time nine years old, and I was about eleven. I remember where she stood, and how she looked; and I can still see her bare feet, her bare head, her brown face, and her short tow-linen frock. She was crying. What it was about, I have long ago forgotten. But it was the tears that preserved the picture for me, no doubt. She was a good child, I can say that for her. She knew me nearly seventy years ago. Did she forget me, in the course of time? I think not. If she had lived in Stratford in Shakespeare's time, would she have forgotten him? Yes. For he was never famous during his lifetime, he was utterly obscure in Stratford, and there wouldn't be any occasion to remember him after he had been dead a week.

"Injun Joe," "Jimmy Finn," and "General Gaines" were prominent and very intemperate ne'er-do-weels in Hannibal two generations ago. Plenty of gray-heads there remember them to this day, and can tell you about them. Isn't it curious that two "town-drunkards" and one half-breed loafer should leave behind them, in a remote Missourian village, a fame a hundred times greater and several hundred times more particularized in the matter of definite facts than Shakespeare left behind him in the village where he had lived the half of his lifetime?

Mark Twain.

www.ingramcontent.com/pod-product-compliance
Lightning Source LLC
Chambersburg PA
CBHW031415250626
47155CB00004B/1494